LONG MOSS

JAMES CESSFORD

CHAPELKILL PRESS

Preface by James Cessford

Some maps have forgotten Chapelkill. You can still find it should you wish. Look for the metal fingerpost on the main road into Whitby. Rooksnest Manor is a little way out from the village, at the foot of the moors. There are few references to the property in the usual gazetteers or guides. This book is perhaps the only comprehensive history of the house that exists.

Those readers familiar with the Chapelkill Press will know we specialise in local stories and accounts. I have a particular interest in this one as I am the current custodian of Rooksnest and what's left of its remarkable collection of books. Restoration of the house is proving stubbornly protracted, and I have made little progress, despite the hundreds of hours devoted to it. The task is beginning to overwhelm me, possessing my waking and my sleeping hours. I remember vividly the sense of triumph upon completing a section of the house, applying the finishing touches, down to the smallest of details, only to find the rooms undone again the following morning. That I am more productive in my dreams is a source of continued frustration for me. It is with weary trepidation I leave the comfort of my caravan every sunrise and trudge along the drive to the house.

But I digress. *Lung Moss* is a portmanteau in three parts. Book one was submitted to us by the protagonist's nephew. We were commissioning an anthology of fishing tales on behalf of the tourist office. Wisely perhaps, they did not consider this story suitable. I acquired the second account at an auction, sight unseen, part of a collection of local maps, architectural plans, and legal documents. Although the writer is now deceased, I thought it prudent to redact his name. The story in book three came to me more directly. It was delivered to Rooksnest Manor by hand, appearing one morning on the side table in my hallway. In a printed note on top of his manuscript the author relinquished both recognition and financial reward, choosing to remain anonymous. He simply wanted his story to be told.

They came to Rooksnest with particular desires - the pursuit of an ancient fish, escape from another life, the acquisition of a rare library. But the house has its own stories. They tell of fungi and standing stones and the cosmic ritual of the Hunt. These tales are older and darker. And soon they will be yours.

James Cessford, Editor, Chapelkill Press

BOOK ONE
THE MILLPOND
(A fisherman's tale)

Foreword by Jacob Taylor

This is Uncle Pete's story, not mine. He and my father were close when I was young. I remember them sitting in the garage for hours, messing about with fishing tackle. Dad talked about fishing much more than he went. It was Uncle Pete who got me into it. Every week in the summer holidays he would take me to the Roman Lakes near Marple. One day he stopped. I didn't know why at the time and my parents would never talk about it. I barely saw him after that. He came round one night when I was in bed. I remember some commotion outside and Dad's raised voice. I peeked through the curtains to see my uncle curled up in a ball on the drive, Dad standing over him. I watched as my father helped him to his feet and ushered him inside. Then it fell quiet. I think Uncle Pete stayed the night on the sofa, but by the time I got up for school in the morning he had gone. He was put in a care home shortly after. I thought those homes were for old people, but my uncle was younger than Dad so I could not understand why he was there. My parents never explained and wouldn't let me go with them to visit.

When I was old enough to drive, I went to see Uncle Pete on my own. Mum was reluctant at first, but she eventually gave me the address, a converted mill in Broadbottom, just outside Glossop. I think it had recently opened when Uncle Pete moved there. It was all air fresheners and bleached floors, a chemical mask over the smell of urine and cabbage. After explaining to the receptionist who I was, he gave me a room number and directions to the third floor.

I knocked on the door several times, but there was no answer. Cautiously I opened it slightly and poked my head inside, hoping my uncle wasn't undressing. Thankfully he was sitting in an armchair looking out through the window.

"Uncle Pete, it's me Jake. Can I come in?" He did not respond. "I'm coming in, hope that's ok."

There was no acknowledgement from my uncle as I stepped into the room and closed the door. It was pleasant enough in there, cleaner and bigger than I had imagined and painted in an unusual pale scarlet. A strange smell hung in the air, unlike that in the hallways and reception. Other than a photograph of Auntie Emma on the bedside cabinet, there were few personal items in the room. It could have been anyone's. My uncle had not stirred before I ran out of things to look at. Then I spotted a kettle next to the TV on the sideboard.

"I'm going to make us a cup of tea."

I set about preparing two cups as noisily as I could, in the hope he would hear me. Still he did not turn around. The kettle took an age to boil, and I stood there awkwardly, staring at the back of my uncle's head. His hair had grown long and pale and was a little matted. Some ten minutes later I had a mug of hot tea in each hand. I took a breath and walked towards the armchair. With every step closer, the compulsion to turn around and go grew stronger. I fought against this urge until I drew level with the side of his chair. From this angle I could make out my uncle's profile. I froze. He was almost unrecognizable. His skin had become grey, the colour of pencil lead, and peeled from his face in dry, cracked scales. Slowly he turned his head towards me. The flesh on his neck popped and splintered, like the cut of a knife through pork crackling. Both cups fell from my hands, and I ran from the room.

I told Mum what happened when I got home, but I never talked about it with my dad. Mum explained that Uncle Pete had developed anaemia, and a fungal infection of the skin. I never visited him again, and now I won't get the chance. Uncle Pete passed away last month.

I am between jobs, so I agreed to help Dad clear his brother's things. The house had stood empty for fifteen years, a time capsule from the day Uncle Pete moved out. It was actually my dad's house. He bought it as an investment and rented it out to my uncle when he and Auntie Emma split up. Dad could not bring himself to find new tenants after Uncle Pete was placed in care. I guess he hoped my uncle would get better one day and return home.

Dad sent me into the attic whilst he worked on the rest of the house. It was stiflingly hot up there and only partially boarded. Thankfully there wasn't much to clear - a box of records, three piles of books, an assortment of ancient-looking camping equipment. Something else was hidden behind the hot water tank. I dropped to my knees and dragged out an old-fashioned portmanteau case. There were clothes in there, a wash bag, a tackle box, and six leather-bound journals. I pulled out the journals and placed them on the floor in front of me. I sat there cross-legged, staring at them, unsure whether it was disrespectful to read them, or not read them. Eventually my curiosity decided, and I selected one at random. It was a record of Uncle Pete's fishing trips, incredibly detailed and beautifully hand-written, with the odd account of his working day, references to his childhood with Dad, and his thoughts about the world. I scanned the dates until I found the entries describing our sessions on the Roman Lakes. My uncle's enthusiasm and joy at taking me fishing filled me with regret for how I had treated him at our last encounter.

The story you are about to read is of my uncle's final fishing trip, about the time he stopped visiting. It is from his most recent journal and appears to be the last thing he wrote. The front and back cover are caked in dry mud, and the pages warped from water damage. Uncle Pete had taken great care to save its contents however, and although the handwriting becomes a little spidery towards the end, it remains legible. Apart from a couple of minor editorial changes in line with my uncle's own annotations, I have presented it exactly as it was written. So it is as true as you can hope, or at least as true as any fisherman's tale.

JT

June 19, Thursday

Helen

I have been spat at, punched in the face, even had a shotgun pointed at me. This was worse. It is easier to do my job in the face of hostility. I can use their aggression to my advantage. When they realise they have exposed themselves to further, more immediate legal action, they generally back down. More than that is how it affects me. It is much easier to take away a person's house from a point of moral high ground, however unstable that ground is. This was worse. She didn't argue, or shout, she just sobbed, her face a smeared mask of make-up, dust, and tears as she carried her baby out in a car seat. This was my third and final call; the day I changed the locks, boarded the windows, and anything left in the house was lost.

"Keep an eye on Nicholas for me."
She placed the car seat on the ground in front of me before I could answer and strode back inside. The baby looked up at me, smiling. I looked away. She came out with a battered red suitcase and loaded it into the trunk of her car.

"I need to find Jack."
"Jack?
"Yes Jack. Jack, my cat."
"Ok miss."

"You can call me Helen you know. That's my name. Helen."

"Ok."

I never use their names. It's easier that way, easier for me. I didn't help her find Jack. I hate cats, partly due to my allergy, but partly because I just hate them. I peered through the kitchen window as the girl disappeared round the back of the house calling Jack's name. Through the grimy glass I could see remains of a life. Some people make a point of leaving their house as messy as they can, others take a weird pride in leaving it spotless. This girl's house was somewhere in the middle, a normal home, frozen in time.

I looked down at the ground below the window. I was standing in a large cluster of toadstools. Those I had not crushed beneath my boots were rather beautiful. Their caps had split and peeled open into rays. They looked like pale flowers, or six-pointed stars fallen from the night. I wiped the sole of my boot on the lawn. Pieces of broken mushroom were mashed into the grip, and I picked them out absently as I watched the girl return clutching a large black cat.

"Hold Jack for me while I put Nicholas in the car." I stared at her. I considered telling her about my allergy, but it felt a little pathetic in the circumstances. Besides, I just wanted her to leave. Whilst I found her sobbing uncomfortable, there had been a subtle shift in the power balance between us that unsettled me even more. I hadn't noticed her size until she stood there in front of me. I am at least average height for a man, and she towered over me. She wasn't physically intimidating, but she had a presence that was difficult to quantify. It was a natural strength, like a tree, or a rock.

"Well?"

"Ok miss."

"Take it!"

She thrust the cat at me and let go. I almost dropped it. This would have no doubt resulted in the cat's escape through the hedgerow, dragging my discomfort out further. I quickly drew my arms towards me and trapped that writhing black mass against my chest. It hissed and struggled violently, but it didn't bite. It did not even manage a scratch.

After securing the baby seat in the car, she marched towards me, grabbed the cat under one arm and went to lock the front door. Before I could tell her that wouldn't be necessary, she let out a short gasp and dropped the keys on the ground. She stood there looking down at them, not moving, not speaking. Several moments passed. Then her free arm began to sway. It was unusually long and moved like weed in a gentle stream. Eventually she looked up.

"Sleep well at night do you Peter?"

She didn't wait for an answer. It is natural for people to behave strangely when they lose something they love. My colleagues recount with glee the bizarre responses they have observed when they take away someone's keys.

What she did next was new. She pointed at me with her left hand and walked backwards to her car, smoothly and effortlessly, not once taking her eyes off mine. After opening the door, she climbed inside with her cat, and skidded off through a cloud of dust and gravel.

The picture

It didn't take long to secure the house. This was the easy bit – new locks, wooden boards on the lower windows, the repossession notice. Then I had to go inside, turn off the gas and water, and check nothing was left plugged in. Some of my colleagues enjoy this part, poking around, assembling a story for the rest of us at the office. I hate it. This is the point when you can't look away, when you must confront what you are doing. Kid's sketches on the fridge, a Polaroid of happier times, letters from a loved one - it's not a persistent debtor you're processing, it's a human being, with hopes and dreams. And you're destroying them.

I moved through the house as quickly and systematically as possible, trying to starve my future dreams of ammunition. There is always something that catches your eye and gets stuck there. In her house it was a large photograph at the end of the hallway, mounted in a bright red frame. I had nearly made it out, and my guard was down. Before I knew it, I had lifted the picture off the wall, leaving behind it a square of vivid paint the sun had been unable to bleach. Printed on the back of the frame was the seller's stamp, *"Dr Wistman's Golden Spindles",* and a woodcut illustration of a shooting star. Beside this was a paper label, handwritten with the words - *The Millpond, Rooksnest Manor, Chapelkill.* I turned the picture over in my hands. It captured a country house with long sloping lawns and trees to one side. In the foreground, taking up most of the shot, was the corner of a pool.

With a single look at that still water, I knew there would be carp in it. It is shameful what I did next. I have never done it before, despite the temptation, but I didn't hesitate. I opened my brief case and slipped the photograph inside. Then I locked up the house, got in my car and drove away.

I have happily lost countless hours chasing giant carp. When Emma and I were together, it had been a cause of conflict, until one day she made me choose. It was a neat bookend to our relationship, as I had taken her to the pool at Lyme Park on our first date. The pool teemed with big roach, but not many carp. The only one you ever saw was a bloated ten pounder, gliding through the murky water like a pale ghost. Fishing pools were the background of other significant points in my life - my first cigarette (menthol, they were better for you), my first alcoholic drink (a warm Skol), my first fight (a story for another time). All these firsts were instigated by Rob. He is my older brother by three years, and I idolised him a little at the time. I miss Rob. He's not dead or anything, he just doesn't fish anymore. He gave up when Jake was born. I always hoped Rob would come fishing again when Jake grew up. He got into golf instead. Golf? What a dick. Ironically, it is Jake that comes with me now. He's a good lad.

Work has taken a greater and greater toll on my self-worth. Without Emma to help me through it, fishing has become more than a hobby. I don't run, I don't use drugs, I fish. In those stolen moments at the water's edge, the rest of the world slips quietly beneath the surface. It is the only time I am truly happy.

This job affords me regular fishing trips, no doubt why I have tolerated it for so many years. You could argue I have fitted my working life around fishing, rather than the other way round. I will volunteer for the most difficult assignments, the ones all the others refuse, if they bring me within casting distance of a favourite pond or lake.

I know the location of all the best-known carp pools, and most of the lesser-known ones too. Some of this knowledge has been collected along the criss-cross paths I have carved across the country with work. The rest I have gleaned from ancient maps pored over in the Reading Room of Manchester's Northcliffe Library. Rooksnest Manor is new to me. I have fished for long enough to recognise a carp pool from a photograph alone – a tangled reed bed, giant lilies, the willow on the bank. This millpond is what I have always dreamed of, a secret pool, the hidden home of that ancient, monster carp.

Fortune has been kind and rewarded me with four days off before my next job. I am unable to find Chapelkill in my atlas, but I remember reading the name on an old wooden sign as I queued in traffic on the drive over from Whitby. The boot of the Volvo is filled with fishing tackle as usual. Instead of returning home to Glossop, I headed back towards the moors.

Chapelkill

Chapelkill was not easy to find. A series of fingerposts led me on a spiralling path along narrow, shaded lanes. The hedgerows on either side climbed above the car, tangling into a thick canopy overhead. I negotiated these tapering green tunnels for almost an hour. Branches grew closer and closer until they rattled angrily against the doors and the roof. The feeling of being unwelcome, of being a trespasser in the landscape, grew into a distinct unease. It became so dark the Volvo's lights automatically brightened. I could have been under the ground by this point and had to fight off rising panic. Turning the car around was impossible so I blindly pressed on. There was a brilliant flash of light as the hedgerows came to a sudden end and the sun streamed down through the windscreen. I blinked and found myself beside a pretty village green. The lane widened out and cottages appeared on either side.

With some relief I abandoned the Volvo in a side street next to the library and set off on foot. I found myself at a market square, crammed with stalls. In the middle was an old well and a large, pyramidal boulder. Meeting the ground at its narrowest point, the boulder sat in a low metal frame. Beside the rock, a small, hand-painted wooden sign stuck out the ground obliquely.

The Bolide Stone
Ring your finger round the stone,
Stone shall linger skin and bone.

I ignored these instructions as I needed to find a room.

The Drab Tooth is tall and narrow. The lower windows are convex, as if something bulges from the pub and onto the street. Outside is a bench, a brush to clean your boots, and a bowl of water for dogs. I decided they must be used to welcoming strangers.

The landlord did not seem keen on me staying "out of season", but I offered to pay up front in cash. Eventually he handed me a key attached to a giant rabbit's foot and directed me up to the third floor. I put my coat on the bed and took a cursory glance around the room. Emma would have turned her nose up at it, but it is adequate enough. Besides, I will only be here for one sleep, I intend to spend tomorrow night by the millpond. There is a desk by the window, so I dumped my briefcase, removed my journal and pen, and returned downstairs.

The lounge is comfortable and inviting. It has a low ceiling and stone flags, and the faint whiff of carbolic and sheep-dip. There are enough people in here to create an atmosphere, but not enough for it to feel crowded. I have never heard of the beers on offer, which is unusual as I have drunk in pubs all over this part of North Yorkshire. I ordered a pint of Dead Man's Fingers. It was particularly good, rich and malty, and it wasn't long before I was onto my second. The landlord turned out to be friendly enough, though conversation proved difficult. He struggled to talk about anything outside the town. He is pale-eyed and has that blank expression men wear when they are assessing you or hiding something. His accent is unusual. There is a northern ring to it, but with a cadence more familiar in the villages of Devon and Cornwall.

An old cane fly rod hangs from a shelf of tankards, and on the bar, between three pickle jars and a cigar tin, is a small glass cabinet. Inside are nine flies, expertly tied with coloured threads. I would try to steer our small talk onto fishing. A secret pool is secret for a reason and no local would readily give up its location to a stranger. I had to tread carefully.

"I'm in town for a couple of days. Can you recommend anything?"
The landlord shrugged. "There's the Bolide Stone."
"What's the story there?"
"It's a large boulder."

"Yeah?"

"It rocks."

"Like a logan?"

"Said to have fallen out the sky."

"Interesting. Though I imagine a meteor that size would leave a mark!"

There followed a period of silence. My attempt to control the conversation was beginning to flounder. I would just have to come out with it.

"What about fishing?"

"What *about* fishing?"

"Are there are any spots you could suggest?"

"No."

"Someone told me about Rooksnest Millpond. Is that nearby?

"Never heard of it."

The landlord closed the discussion and moved to the end of the bar to clean some glasses. That was it. A total denial is as good as confirmation the millpond is close by and worth fishing. I excused myself and asked the landlord where the gents were. He nodded towards the cigarette machine and returned to his glass-cleaning.

Red Cage

The toilet is dominated by an enormous glass cabinet attached to the wall beside the hand towel. Inside the cabinet is a monster carp. It is easily a metre in length and some 60cm in depth, a 50 pounder at least, maybe more. Patchy scaling suggests a mirror carp, but I have never seen one like this before. The carp's head and dorsal fin are a dull grey, like pencil lead, and along its flank is a grid of hexagonal red scales, creating a raised lattice pattern on its skin. Equally unusual is its forehead, which bulges forward over its eyes, almost a horn. In the centre of the fish's belly is a large circular scar. Although possibly a clumsy slip from the taxidermist, the scar appears to have healed naturally. The ring of small perforations suggests the bite mark of a giant lamprey.

The cabinet is designed to make the fish look alive and the impression it creates is incredible. You can sense the moving water, the swaying reeds, the gold shimmer of that giant fish. Why it is consigned to the gents I cannot imagine. A brass plaque is attached to the bottom of the wooden frame – *"Red Cage, trapped 1908 by Alfred Woo…, Rooksn…"* Some of the inscription is scratched away, obscuring the location. But I know where it is. I pissed as quickly as two pints would allow and returned to the bar.

"That's quite a fish."
The landlord looked at me blankly.
"In the gents."
"You mean Red Cage?"
"That's it. She's a monster. What is she 50, 60 pounds?"
"Aye, a monster."
"I've never seen a carp like it."

"You don't want to."

"Well it's magnificent, and beautifully presented."

"Don't know about that. Stuck here now though."

The landlord's expression suddenly changed, suggesting the moment was lost. I had to try.

"Where was she caught?"

"I don't recollect."

"Could it have been the millpond?"

"There ain't no millpond!"

And with that, my chance slipped away. Defeated, I picked up my beer and retired to a table in the corner. I sunk another pint as I wrote up the day's events in my journal. I think I can manage one more if I order some food.

Elizabeth

Nursing that pint for an hour or so, I skimmed through the *Chapelkill Messenger*, looking for clues. I reached the back page, the results of last week's hen races, without finding a reference to Rooksnest Manor or the millpond. I returned to the culture section in the centre spread. The Split Gill on the other side of the market promoted its bill for this weekend's Solstice Festival. Supported by the Goathland Plough Stots, tomorrow's headline act is ABC/DC - *"Lancashire's premier covers band will be playing AC/DC songs in the style of ABC. You haven't heard Heatseeker until you've heard it the way Martin Fry would sing it."*

"Will you be eating with us sir?"

Engrossed in the festival line-up, I visibly jumped when she spoke. I looked up at her and she smiled back at me, amused by my reaction. Her hair was long and black, and she had the most fascinating eyes. She had a smell too, unusual, but wonderful, something like a new book. Writing this down, only hours later, I struggle to capture any more of her on the page. I remember finding her quite beautiful, but hers was like a face glimpsed in a dream and only the feeling of her remains.

I coughed and composed myself.

"What do you recommend?"

"You'll enjoy the pie."

"What kind of pie is it?

"Meat."

"Do you know what kind of meat it is?"

Instead of answering she laughed and studied me with the same look of amusement. Several seconds of silence passed and I realised this was the only response I would get.

"The pie it is then. Oh, and another pint please."

"Very good sir."

Then she did something unusual. She took my left hand in hers and began stroking it. I hadn't felt a woman's touch for some time and didn't know how to react.

"You been picking toadstools?"

She lifted my hand and held the back of it in front of my face. In the middle was a hexagonal patch of red skin, raised like eczema and about the size of a fifty pence piece. That fucking cat.

"They can do that to a man."

I nodded, uncertain if I had spoken aloud or not. She let go of my hand and I watched her turn round and walk back towards the bar. I rubbed the mark and it tingled slightly.

As I waited for my pie to arrive, it dawned on me the waitress was more likely to share the location of the millpond. Perhaps I was jumping to conclusions, but she did not look like any carp fisherman I had met. The pie arrived quickly, and I took my chance.

"Could you bring me the salt please?"

"There's no salt."

Whilst this seemed a little unusual, I did not want to fall out with her.

"Oh, okay. Can I ask you something?"

"That depends on the question."

"Do you know Rooksnest Manor?"

Another expression flashed briefly across her dark eyes, but she held her smile.

"'Fraid not sir."

She is either well coached by the landlord, or the millpond didn't exist after all.

"Ok, thank you anyway."

"I hear you're looking to fish."

"Yes, if I can find somewhere."

"You don't look like the hunter."

"I wouldn't call myself that."

"We don't always get to choose."

"Er, no, I guess not."

"Betty and Issac will know."

"Know what?"

"Where the pool is."

"Ok, great, are they here?"

Elizabeth laughed but did not explain the joke.

"Have you looked at the map?"

"The map?"

"Behind you." And with that she walked away.

I turned around. It was huge, I don't know how I missed it when I sat down. So as not to draw suspicion from the landlord, I ignored the map and set about eating my pie. It was delicious, even without salt.

"Elizabeth … Elizabeth! … Come out here. I've got to change the barrel."

This was my chance. The waitress came out from the kitchen as the landlord dragged open the hatch and disappeared down the cellar. At once the bar crowded with men. With everyone otherwise distracted, I stood up and surveyed the map behind me. Hand drawn and particularly well-detailed, it showed the library, the market square, the Bolide Stone, the well, and the pub, highlighted with the words *"Your Here"*. Even the map and the fish in the toilet had a reference in the key. There was a familiar pattern to the village's shape, but I couldn't determine what it brought to mind. Then I found what I was looking for. It was some way out from the village, on the edge of the moors. I flicked to the last page of my journal and wrote the directions down in comprehensive steps that will be easy to follow in the morning. If I leave the Drab Tooth at cockscrike I'll be at the millpond and fishing by five thirty.

The Phenomenon

I tried in vain to finish the pie, but its size and density, as well as my excitement at finding the millpond, had me beaten. I felt guilty for not cleaning the plate, both the pastry and the unspecified meat had been exceptional. With the landlord now back up from the cellar, Elizabeth came over to clear the table.

"How was the pie sir?"

"Excellent, thank you."

"Now I wonder what you'll be wanting for afters?"

"Would I be able to buy a bottle of scotch and take it upstairs?"

I unfolded my wallet, crammed full of notes, pulled out twenty pounds and handed it to Elizabeth. She took it without looking.

"Of course, celebrating are we?"

My neck and cheeks flushed.

"Something like that."

"Get on your way if you want sir, I'll bring it up for you."

"Ok, thank you, that's very kind."

After several hours in the bar, my room was further from the ground than I remembered. I climbed more stairs than it seemed possible to fit between three floors and was breathing heavily when I stumbled through the door. The room is basic but clean. There is a desk and chair tucked beneath the window, a large wooden wardrobe, a double bed, and an en-suite. A single picture hangs from the wall, a small ink sketch of what looks like a white star with a thousand black rays, or the spore print of some giant mushroom. It is pleasing to the eye and unusually soothing. Attached to the bottom of the frame is a metal plaque – *The Phenomenon*.

I opened my briefcase and removed the photograph of the millpond to study its layout. To the uninitiated, coarse fishing will make little sense. If you are not eating your prey, why bother? For me it's the hunt, the preparation, the moments away from the water, planning, dreaming. There are lilies in the centre of the pool, a willow tree dragging its branches in the water, and what appears to be the edge of a boathouse. I notice two figures on the lawn. One looks to be a man sat cross-legged beneath a stone folly; the other is a woman, blurred as if running. A loud knocking startles me, and I slip the picture under the bedspread.

"Just a minute."

I unlocked the door to find Elizabeth standing outside holding a tray. I stood there for a time staring at her, not speaking.

"May I come in?"

"Yes, of course, sorry."

I stepped to one side and watched Elizabeth carry the tray over to the desk beneath the window. After slowly removing a bottle of scotch, a six-sided tumbler glass and an ice bucket, she turned towards me and nodded at the bed.

"Am I in there?"
She watched me with amusement as I struggled to find the right words. Following several seconds of awkward silence, she eventually let me go.

"In your book."
I looked down at my open journal on the bed cover.

"Er, no, it's just a fishing diary," I lied. She continued to smile at me.

"Are we looking after you sir?"

"Yes, you've been excellent, thank you."

"And the landlord?"

"Well he's a little surly, but he grows on you."
The alcohol and the perceived intimacy of our conversation made me a little more candid than I intended.

"I'm sorry to hear that. He's never quite played his part here."

"It's no problem at all. And don't worry, I won't tell him you said that."

"You may tell him whatever you wish sir. Will you be wanting anything else?"

"No, that will be all, thank you."
She stood there looking at me, not moving, not speaking.

"Of course, sorry." I fumbled around with my wallet, drew out a five-pound note and held it towards her.

"That won't be necessary sir."

A little embarrassed once again, I slipped the note into my pocket and watched her walk across the room.

"Well, thank you again for everything."

"Thank *you* sir."

She turned round as she closed the door.

"Sleep well Peter."

Then she laughed and was gone.

After putting on pyjamas and brushing my teeth, I fished around in my wash bag and pulled out two pairs of scissors, one for my hair and beard, and a smaller one for nails. I cut the nails on three fingers from each hand only, as I need to keep some length on my thumbs and forefingers to help with knots. Clippings ricocheted round the room like bullets in a gun fight. I did not bother picking them up. Although the carpet looks clean enough, I don't want to happen across fragments of other people. I trimmed my beard and hair in front of the mirror over the sink. When I pulled out the plug, the water sat stagnant in the bowl before it finally seeped down, leaving my hair pasted to the sides. Again, this isn't my problem. Once I considered myself presentable, I poured a generous scotch, got into bed, and wrote the rest of the evening up in my journal.

At some point I fell asleep. I woke up slumped forward, journal in my lap, empty scotch glass overturned on the bed beside me. It was a warm evening and I had left the window open. Laughter and exaggerated whispers carried up into my room from the market square below. I turned off the lamp on the nightstand and climbed down from my bed. Concealing myself ineffectively behind the curtain, I peered out through the window.

The noise came from three women circling the Bolide Stone. Two of them were standing up with their backs towards me, laughing at the third who was squatting behind the boulder urinating. They continued to giggle and whisper until one of them turned around. It was Elizabeth, the waitress. She waved slowly and I instinctively waved back, partially hidden by the drape. Her hand came down and she began to unbutton her top, our eyes still locked. After sliding out the last button she gently pulled open her shirt. Beneath it was another shirt, identical to the first. She started to unbutton that one and I was struck by the notion this might go on forever, that it might be shirts all the way down. The woman obscured by the Bolide Stone straightened her clothes and stood up suddenly to face me. I gasped and dropped to the floor. It was her, the girl I evicted yesterday. Tall and strong, like a tree. The three of them laughed as I lay there. They continued laughing as I crawled over to the bed, climbed inside, and pulled the covers over my head.

June 20, Friday

Dr Wistman's Golden Spindles

When I awoke this morning there was a hangover waiting for me behind the eyes. The sun streamed in through the thin curtains, and I realised I had overslept. I looked at my watch and leapt out of bed. It was 8.30, damn it! My clothes were no longer in a messy pile on the floor where I left them, but neatly folded over the back of the chair. My journal, which I had closed and placed on the floor beside the bed, was on the desk, open. Someone has been in the room whilst I slept. I grabbed my wallet from my trouser pocket and quickly counted the notes. They were all there. I imagined Emma then, shaking her head at me, disappointed by my instinctive distrust of other people.

After a couple of glasses of water, I began to relax. A later arrival was probably for the best. The occupants of Rooksnest Manor were unlikely to welcome me at five in the morning, however much I offered them to let me fish. Besides, this is the longest day of the year, and I will not be short of light. Hopefully I'll see dawn at the pool tomorrow.

As well as folding my clothes, someone had tidied the room and cleaned my hairs out the sink. I brushed my teeth and stared vacantly into the bathroom mirror. Last night's unusual episode came back to me like a dream. I spat out a mouthful of blood-streaked toothpaste, dried my face, and quickly wrote the events down in my journal before they slipped away again. Looking down at my hand, I see the rash has grown larger and redder. It is also beginning to itch.

I dressed and gathered my things. The bottle of scotch was three quarters full, so I slipped it into my briefcase. I keep a thermos flask in there, and there was tea-making paraphernalia on the desk. The kettle was tiny and took two frustratingly long boils to fill my flask with hot water.

Checking out of the inn was without incident. The landlord was in a better mood, and I made no mention of Rooksnest, pretending instead I was off to Whitby for the day. I had avoided going down for breakfast. Despite having written off last night's events as a dream, I was uneasy at the prospect of running into Elizabeth again. Unwilling to send me away hungry, the landlord prepared me a packed lunch, or *docky*, as he called it – six hard-boiled eggs, a large pork pie, two apples, and an enormous slab of fruit cake. It was very kind, and I left the pub in good spirits.

I had parked the Volvo in a side street on the other side of the town square. The market was in full swing, selling all manner of foods, remedies, hardware, and such. It felt a wasted opportunity not to try the Bolide Stone, so I gently drew a circle on it with the end of my finger as the sign instructed. The boulder immediately tipped on its point, striking the sides of the hexagonal metal frame around its base. Six notes repeated themselves, ringing like bells beneath the ground. My head swam and I grabbed at the rock as it fell away into darkness. The sun became the moon and the market emptied. I blinked and the turn passed as quickly as it arrived. I became aware of a stallholder watching me, and the faint whiff of piss. Above the stallholder's head hung a familiar hand-painted sign – *"Dr Wistman's Golden Spindles"*. Immediately conscious of the stolen picture in my briefcase, I hurried guiltily to the car.

Mad honey

The map in the pub proved at first to be accurate, and the single-track lane off the road into Whitby was where it ought to be. The lane was far longer than it had been drawn though, and started to climb heavily, almost taking me up onto the moors. About to turn back, I spotted an imposing pair of iron gates, set back slightly from the bend of a sharp left turn. There was just enough room to reverse the Volvo in front.

The gates were locked shut with a padlock and a thick rusting chain. The metalwork was decoratively smithed into a woodland scene with a wooden sign attached in the middle – *"The Rooksnest Foundation."* Below this, smaller letters, peeling from the sign read, *"Foundation Director – Dr Cullis. Operated and managed by the Chapelkill*

Medical Trust". I peered through the gate down the gently sloping drive. Although the estate's rhododendron bushes had grown out of control and covered much of the grounds, I could make out the top floor of the house, the house in the photograph.

The wall on either side of the gate was some seven feet tall. I raised my foot onto the highest horizontal bar I could comfortably reach and pulled myself up. I had a clear view of the estate from there. Clumps of rhododendron, hawthorn trees, and heather made a fortress of the house, which was further secured by boards and planks on the windows and door. The land dipped, obscuring the millpond, and beyond that thick woodland climbed up the side of the moors. I looked down at the ground on the other side of the wall. It was a little uneven, *Charlie-drunk-grass* my nan used to call it, but it looked safe enough to land on. At eye level, tied to the top of the gate were two more signs, smaller and handwritten – *"Danger Marshland's"* and *"Guard Dog's - Keep Out"*. I smiled. The cavalier use of apostrophes would have irritated Emma.

After climbing down from the gate, I removed the picture from my briefcase to help decide on a suitable swim. Somewhere near the boathouse looked good. There were enough trees behind to obscure me from the fish, but no overhanging branches to tangle my line. From there I could drop a ledger to the edge of the lily pads. There is something else in the picture I failed to notice last night.

On the second floor of the house is the figure of a man, standing at the window. I slipped the picture back into my briefcase and opened the boot.

Over the last decade or so, fishing has become a military operation for many, especially carp anglers. They tool themselves up as if going into a war zone, where fish are the enemy to be mercilessly hunted and captured. Whilst guilty of the odd nod to this weaponised approach, I have stripped my kit down to its essentials. My holdall contains two rods, a telescopic net, a fold-up stool, a groundsheet, and a fishing umbrella with overwrap. In my oversized satchel I keep tackle, bait, cigarettes, scales, a radio, camera, knife, and blanket. I filled the rest of the satchel with the food provided by the landlord, the bottle of scotch, and my flask of tea.

I emptied my rod holdall and squeezed its contents between the bars of the gate. To avoid carrying them, I wore the old, knitted gansey and the wax jacket I keep in the boot. Although it is hot now, I will be glad of these when the sun goes down. I pulled the strap of the bulging satchel over my shoulder and across my chest and mounted the gate. There was another horizontal bar slightly higher up. From that bar it was relatively easy to transfer myself onto the top of the wall. I sat up there for a minute and looked around, my heart beating faster than usual. Life had built to this moment, from the first time Rob showed me how to cast a line. I was almost laughing when

I pushed my feet against the wall and dropped to the ground.

At some point during that short fall, my satchel swung out to the side, throwing me off balance. I struck the ground awkwardly, turning my left ankle, and cursing loudly. I clutched my foot through the boot, conscious that if I took it off, it might not go back on again. Gripping the gate, I pulled myself up and gingerly leaned into the pain. I winced a little, but it was by no means excruciating. Emma would have laughingly told me to man up. Once I was at the pool and set up, I would be ok, as I'd be sitting down for much of the day after that. I can worry about getting back over the gate tomorrow. Slowly I gathered the contents of my holdall and slid them back inside before setting off along the drive.

Weeds pushed their way up through the gravel, and brakes of rhododendron reduced the drive to a series of narrow, buzzing canyons. Swarms of midges and bees and horse flies crackled the air with the vibration of a thousand tiny wings. The bushes' flowers were in full bloom, creating a kaleidoscope of purples, whites, and yellows. The aroma was overwhelming, a sickly, intoxicating blend of sugars and spices that left me light-headed. Rob once told me why nature guides classified honey made from rhododendron as poisonous. He insisted *poisonous* was the convention used for classifying psychosomatic substances, and Mad Honey, as it was known, could make you hallucinate.

Despite the uneven patchwork of boards and planks, Rooksnest is an attractive Georgian house. A long-handled felling axe leaned against the wall, so I thought it prudent to make enquiries. I hobbled carefully up three steps to the planked-up door. The stone slabs bowed in the middle and were dusted with wooden splinters. At the top, on either side, two giant stone rooks stood guard, their heads turned to observe visitors. The doorway was visible through a gap in the planks, so I reached my hand inside and tugged on the bell. Wire scraped from the hole with a dissonant shriek, before snapping back again violently like a bolt gun. A series of bells tinkled somewhere deep inside the house. Beneath this was the faint patter of feet – rats, or cats, foxes even. I did not wait long. Meeting someone was only likely to decrease my chances of fishing.

A hawthorn tree

Attached to the left of the house is a small walled garden, so I went round the other way, across the rear lawn. In contrast to the state of the drive and the boarded-up windows, the lawn is surprisingly well-kept. A copse of six ash trees flanks one side of the garden, and on the other stand three giant stones, with a fourth perched on top, the folly from the photograph. There are neat beds of irises, yarrow, and lavender, and the freshly cut lawn is tiered down towards woodland at the back of the estate. Trees curl around the pool, obscuring it from me along the oblique angle at which I approached. With every step I grew more nervous. What if the millpond had become a flosh, stagnant and overgrown with reeds? What if the fish had been carried away by disease, or worse? I'd heard stories of great floods overwhelming carp pools and flushing the fish out onto the land.

The sun was already hot enough to split the trees, and I sweated uncomfortably beneath my winter layers. Pain nagged at my ankle and the fishing tackle hung heavier and heavier on my shoulders. I stopped to readjust the satchel and my heart dropped. A gap in the trees had emerged. There was no millpond behind it. There was no water, no lilies, no willows, just a miry hollow. My dream had come to an end, and I felt as if I might cry. Then the marsh began to change. I could not determine what I was seeing as it shifted and swirled. Slowly it moved towards me. When it broke free of the trees I realized. The spew was a trick, an illusion created by the sunlight streaming down through a great cloud of spores. I have never seen anything like it. It was a different hue from yew pollen, and too late in the year. It must have been mushrooms, hundreds, perhaps thousands of them dispersing at once in the woodland beyond the pool. This amber mist swept up the lawn and engulfed me. My skin tingled like static or sunburn. For a moment I could not see or hear. Then it was gone. And my heart leapt with joy.

The wind that brought the spores carried with it that wonderful smell of old, still water. Beneath this were other invisible markers – the scent of honeysuckle, foxglove and elder. There is an atmosphere around carp pools that is difficult to describe, but immediately recognisable. The air is somehow thicker, bloating your lungs like the belly of that monster carp beneath the surface. I struggled across the lawn and the gap in the trees opened slowly until at last I could see the boathouse. The stolen photograph inside my briefcase came to life. With every step forward, the millpond revealed herself. She was beautiful, she was everything I had dreamed of.

The pool is elliptical in shape, some eighty yards across at its widest point, and half that in the other direction. In the centre is a bed of giant water lilies with pockets of reeds dug into the banks. There is not another soul in sight. I do not wish to paint myself as a misanthrope, but the presence of other people is the only thing that could cast a pall on this place.

There is a small dam at the near end of the pool, and collapsing into the opposite corner is an old boathouse, made inaccessible from the lawn by a giant, overgrown rhododendron that has erupted from the woods behind and gripped the water's edge. This forced me to walk round the pool widdershins. A sunwise turn is preferable if you want to be lucky with the fish, but I had to disregard superstition on this occasion.

Apart from a few stumbles where tree roots burst through the ground, the path around the pool is in good shape. You could fish anywhere, but I had already decided the boathouse at the end would be the best swim. As I lug my fishing tackle along the path, I become aware of something from the corner of my eye. Two faces watch me from between the trees. I jump backwards in surprise before laughing awkwardly. Thick knots of briar tendrils are dragging the two statues back into the woods, and only their heads are visible through the leaves. She is particularly good-looking with prominent cheekbones, wide eyes, and long flowing hair. He is handsome in that military way, with a thick Kitcheneresque moustache, a proud jutting chin, and an intimidating stare. White lichen clings to his face like a death mask.

A few yards on from the statues, an old willow tree weeps into the pool. It would be an attractive spot to set up if not fraught with overhead snags. Besides, I had already made up my mind. Beyond the willow tree, woodland pushes out into the pool, and the path is blocked by a lone sentry, a giant hawthorn coming into bloom. Its leaves are a rich, dark green and those tiny white flowers emerge from the tree as stars in the night sky. I keep a knife in my tackle box, so I pulled it out and hacked at the branches. Rob and I used to call them bread-and-cheese trees and we'd nibble on the leaves when we were young. If you catch them early enough, they have a soft, nutty taste. I tried one for nostalgia's sake, but it had already turned bitter. I spat it out again, retching slightly. *Hawthorn bloom and elder flower fill the house with evil power.*

The hawthorn was too dense to thin out with my blade and I considered whether to turn back, having passed a number of spots suitable to fish. Then I heard it. Folk talk of Mozart, or a baby's laughter, or the crunch of your feet in fresh snow, but that heavy slap of a tail fin on a pool's surface is the most beautiful sound there is. My head turns instinctively towards the millpond, and I catch the gold flash of a giant carp between the lily pads and the boathouse.

There was nothing to do but keep going. At the bottom of the bush is a hare gate, running through to the other side. I could be the hare. Rob and I had squiggled through countless hedges when we were boys, and not only to reach remote fishing spots. We would force our way onto the fairway of the local golf club to collect stray balls from the rough, selling them back to the golfers who'd lost them. This was no different. I put my rod holdall on my left shoulder, waterside, so as not to snag it. Then I removed my satchel and held it out before me like a riot shield. I expected some protest from the branches, but they yielded with ease. They were almost welcoming, as if the hawthorn were using its limbs to draw me gently in. The heart of the tree was silent and black as pitch. And then I was through.

Straightening the holdall and satchel on my shoulders, I realized how dirty I was. The tree has left me painted in mud, from my boots up to the waistband of my trousers. It also took my cap. It hung from the bush at such an angle, it appeared someone was hiding within. I tried to squeeze back into the hawthorn, but the branches were impossibly rigid from this side. Instead, I leaned against the tree and grabbed my cap at full stretch, before cursing loudly and dropping it into the pool. I yanked my arm out to find a silvery thorn sunk into the rash on the back of my left hand. It protruded from the skin by a centimetre or so.

As I teased the thorn out with my knife, the feeling of being watched suddenly formed at the back of my neck. I looked up and out over the millpond. A man had appeared on the lawn. Neither of us moved. After several moments with our gazes locked, I slowly raised my hand to wave. He lowered his head and his eyes flashed silver. His antlers had been obscured by the reflection of the sun in one of the house's lower windows. The stag sniffed something on the breeze before turning his giant head and crossing slowly over the garden until he disappeared from sight. I looked down at my hand. Blood trickled over my fingers and dripped onto the bank. I grabbed my stuff and continued along the path to the boathouse where I wrapped a hanky clumsily around the wound. A trail of red dots has followed me from the hawthorn.

Rook, rook get out of my sight

I arrange my set-up in a neat line on the bank in front of me and inspect it carefully – rod, reel, lead weight, swivel, link, hook, bait. I piece the rod together snugly, grip the reel in place and thread the line up through the rings. After sliding the weight onto the end of the line I secure it with a swivel. Through the eye, six turns round, into the loop and tighten. I am trying a new link between swivel and hook. It is black and braided, and though thicker than fishing line, it softens in water, becoming imperceptible to the fish. Through the eye, six turns round, into the loop and tighten. At the end of the link, I tie on a size four hook. Through the eye, six turns round, into the loop and tighten. I have brought a variety of baits to entice the carp - sweetcorn, pork luncheon meat, tinned new potatoes, and cat biscuits. I decide on a new potato and turn it onto the hook.

Before casting out, I launch two handfuls of sweetcorn over to the lilies. I have recently treated myself to a new catapult. It is accurate at great distances with certain projectiles, but the pouch is not designed for sweetcorn and much of it sprayed across the pool in different directions. This was no matter. I always make an offering to the pool before I start fishing, a tribute if you will. I flick the weight out a little shy of the lily pads. For good measure, I carve off five luncheon meat cubes and fire them out to the same spot with satisfying accuracy.

Everyone uses electronic bite alarms these days. The line slides through a sensor attached to your rod rest and it sets off a bleeper when you get a bite. It seems like cheating to me. If you can't be bothered watching your rod when you're fishing, you shouldn't be fishing. You should find another hobby, like golf. I use two wooden rod rests cut from forked ash branches. Druids favoured the straight grain of ash for their wands, and sickly children were cured in the cleft of the tree's trunk. I hope some of this magic rubs off. To give myself a fighting chance, I draw a little slack from my reel and fold a rectangle of tin foil over the hanging line. There is nothing so wonderful as that silver flash when a swallowed hook pulls it tight.

The umbrella is a pain in the arse to set up as usual and made harder by the handkerchief tied about my hand. The wrapover turns the umbrella into a kind of shit tent - a tent with no front, a gap at the bottom, and a pole right through the middle. It's called a bivvy and only really works if there is no wind, rain falls at the correct angle, and the sun doesn't move in the sky. In spite of this, once I am set up and sitting down, my stuff organised around me, it is the single most beautiful place in the world; the place I feel safest, and happiest, and most at peace.

Once I had taken care of essentials, I stripped off the winter layers and pulled out my journal. Now at last it is time to eat. I am here, beside the perfect pool, eating hard boiled eggs. This is the world. Nothing else matters. Not my job, not Emma, not my swollen ankle or my fucked-up hand. Nothing. I wash three eggs down with a cup of tea. There is something luxurious about a hot drink when you're fishing. It's like it shouldn't be possible. I savour every plasticky sip as I write up this morning's events in my journal.

The manor house is living up to its name, and a clamour of rooks rises from the ash trees. They circle the pool in ever decreasing spirals, before returning noisily to their nests. Fishermen consider this windin' an omen of rain, but I can't see it. The sky is dintless, an unbroken blue canopy joining the horizons. After a short while, three of the more curious birds swoop down onto the lawn and hop towards the pool's edge. They watch me as I write, chattering to themselves. A loud buzzing distracts my gaze, and I follow the flight of a mason bee clutching a stalk of grass like a tiny witch on her broomstick.

The carp that rose earlier has not returned. Except for the occasional boiling, there is no obvious sign of feeding. Big fish can be lethargic in this heat, basking lazily in the weeds rather than looking for food. Or it could be my presence on the bank is still registering as something new, something to be cautious of. Either way, it is barely midday; there's plenty of time for the fish to forget about me and for the weather to turn.

One reliable way to get a bite is lighting up. Big carp instinctively know when you're distracted. This is one of many excuses I have for smoking when I'm fishing. Repelling midges is another. My cigarette fails to entice a carp, but it brings the pool to vivid life - the water's gentle heartbeat, the scented breath of citrus and musk, the metallic spark of dragonflies. The millpond is more beautiful than I could have imagined. Such pools only exist in dreams, or in whispered tales after last orders, when a fisherman's guard is loosened by drink. Rob would have loved this place once upon a time. And Emma. She did come fishing with me on occasions, quite a few, many more times than I shared with her the things she loved doing.

Across the pool, the house looks different to the one I inquired at this morning. The rear walls are unrendered in places, their stone more roughly hewn. It is likely a much older building once stood here, worked and reworked into the house standing here today. A window on the second floor is bricked up behind the glass. They call it a "blind eye" in this part of Yorkshire, a response to the window tax of the nineteenth century. It occurs to me that those responsible for securing the property from intruders have not completed their task. The back of Rooksnest is unprotected; there are no boards or planks of any kind blocking potential entrance points. This is a lazy approach and will earn you a write-up in my office.

This lack of effort makes my view across the pool all the more captivating. It is easy to imagine how the occupants of Rooksnest might have lived – a morning stroll in the woods, lunch on the lawn beside the folly, a spot of fishing until sunset. Lucky beggars.

Basket stinkhorn

Until now the pool has been lythe, with no let up from the sun. At last a gentle breeze blows crossways, cockling the water's surface. My lost cap drifts across the millpond, red and polyester and out of place. It gives the impression of its attachment to someone's head, someone walking across the bottom of the pool. It stops and starts and changes directions, as if the submerged figure is negotiating underwater hazards. Eventually it drifts into the lilies where it still waits.

Although the breeze provides some relief from the merciless heat, it is making precise casting more difficult. I am fixated on a spot just in front of the lily pads. Whilst the water around it is ruffled by wind, this small, square section of the pool remains calm. Its stillness makes it darker than the rest of the millpond, as if a large black box floats below the surface. I have tried again and again to cast into it, but every time the wind picks up my line at the last second and flicks it to one side or the other.

The pain in my hand and foot is starting to nag. I dug out the bottle of scotch, flicked the dregs of tea from my cup and poured a measure, for medicinal purposes you understand. At some point, the strain in my ankle will make standing difficult. Before the anaesthetic effects of the whisky wear off, I'm going to do some stalking with a float.

My second rod is shorter, giving me freedom to roam the banks and get in amongst the trees. The line on this reel is much lighter, 3.5lb, and I have tied on a smaller hook. I use this set-up when I'm not fishing for carp; usually it's for bream or chub, but right now I'm looking for a tench. The water is calmer around the edges, so I'm using a waggler with a long antenna. It's a little sensitive for tench as they tend to play with the bait before they take it, however its extended tip is good for detecting lift bites.

Whilst tench will snap at sweetcorn, they naturally feed on worms. I don't usually fish worms as they attract eels, and reeling one in can spook the carp. But the carp don't appear interested. I have not brought any worms with me, so I'm going to venture into the woodland behind the pool and see if I can dig any out from the ground. I think I'll have another nip of scotch first, to help me on my way.

From a track beside the boathouse, I crossed over the border of trees. The path twisted and dipped and climbed; it turned back on itself and widened and narrowed. When I stopped to give my ankle a rest, I found myself in the heart of a giant wood, thick with elder trees, hornbeam, alder, and hawthorn. The green canopy rippled in the wind, dappling a pattern of light and dark on the ground. It was another pool. I was in the water and on the water, its surfaces above and below. Wildflowers bloomed where the sun came in – cowslip, bluebell, and fool's parsley.

I carried on and the light grew thinner. Eventually I was leaf-whelmed, even on such a bright day. A storm or disease had planted deadfall in the undergrowth that was rotting and damp and carpeted with wood ear mushrooms. The mossy ground was spongy, a good spot to dig for worms. I crouched down and something jumped into the corner of my eye. Recoiling quickly, I looked up to see a great toad sitting on the log, holding my gaze without blinking. After a time, it let me go and gobbled up a bug from the wet bark. The trunk was covered in witches' butter, that yellow, gloopy fungus that oozes from dead wood. I tried to ignore it, but every so often the toad rubbed its chin in that gold scoom, and my stomach turned.

It didn't take long to pull five chunky worms from the damp soil. I had forgotten to bring a tub, so I slipped the worms into my jacket and headed back to the pool. After a minute or so following the track to the boathouse, I realised the woods were growing darker. On my journey here, I had kept to the same path. Although it had meandered in different directions, there had been no branches or junctions. So I turned around and went back the other way. Still the trees above me thickened. Somehow I was lost.

Eventually the path began to curve. With the sun obscured by the tree tops it was difficult to be sure, but it felt as if I were spiralling through the woods in ever-decreasing circles. I kept walking nonetheless, and at some point, the canopy began to thin. Sunbeams pierced the tree tops in narrow shafts, leaving a trail on the dark path. I followed those crumbs of light and the path opened out, until I found myself in a small clearing. A dry log stuck out from between the trees and made a comfortable bench. It was a giant elm, felled by disease. Patches of bark were stripped away, revealing complex systems of miniature tunnels in the trunk. Despite the slow death inflicted by the beetles, their galleries were quite beautiful, conjuring multi-rayed suns and mysterious undersea creatures. They were miniature geoglyphs, the Nazca lines observed from the stars.

The clearing burst with sweet colours – anemones, foxgloves, and nightshade; it wasn't the worst place to lose your bearings. I held my breath to catch a sound from the pool. The woods sung with thrushes and cuckoos, and the gentle rustle of branches. But they were muffled, the trees insulating me from the world beyond. I tried my nose instead. Beyond the glade was a trace of mint, wild garlic and maybe a hint of the pool's ancient water. Something else was confusing my senses, a little like spoiled meat. I stood up from the log and walked out from beneath the trees. In the centre of the clearing was a large ring of mushrooms. They were basket stinkhorn, intricate latticed domes of perfect red hexagons. Their structure brought to mind the giant golf ball radars squatting on the nearby moors.

The centre of the glade opened to the sky. With no canopy overhead, sounds were a little clearer and I could make out the cry of rooks from the ash trees beside the pool. Then another noise began to rise, a faint but growing rustling. I listened as it grew louder. It was the trample of sticks and leaves. Something was charging through the trees, charging towards me. I hobbled quickly across the clearing and scrambled up onto a log. With that, the undergrowth on the other side burst open. At first it appeared nothing had emerged, but when I looked down at the ground it was alive. It was slithering with eels, hundreds upon hundreds of dark eels. They filled the clearing in a second, transforming it into a bubbling, black hole. Just as quickly they were gone.

Eel migration on land is not uncommon at night, after heavy rain. To see one in daylight, in such dry conditions, is surely once in a lifetime. A sudden joy overtook me, a reminder that whatever you think you understand about the world, it is stranger and more wonderful than you can ever know.

I lit a cigarette to celebrate, savouring every long drag. An idea came to me as smoke trickled from my nose. There was only one place the eels could be going and that was the millpond. All I had to do was follow their path. Getting good ideas, this is another reason to smoke. Although the undergrowth had sprung back up, the eels had left their mark, a trail of thick, dark ooze. If you have ever removed one from your hook, you'll be familiar with the sticky brown mucus they leave on your skin.

A doctor fish

The eels had not kept to the path. Following those crusty streaks of drying slime dragged me through patches of gorse and bracken, and the occasional unyielding blackthorn tree. With my weak ankle, it was like pulling myself from a bog in places. By the time I emerged beside the boathouse I was exhausted. Still, it had given me the opportunity to gather armfuls of bone-dry cramble. It will make excellent firewood when the sun starts to dip. After dropping the sticks in a pile, I sat down beneath the bivvy and caught a breath, scratching absently on the bottom of my leg. I rolled up my trousers to find a tick burrowing itself into my calf. Using the tweezers from my tackle box I carefully extracted it from the skin. Its legs twitched as I crushed it between the pointed metal tips. The little bastard. I rewarded myself with another hard-boiled egg, a thin slice of fruit cake, and a nip of scotch.

My ankle is growing sorer. If I want to get on the float, I need to do it soon. I reached into my pocket to grab a worm. There was only one left. In the corner of the pocket is a small hole, on the inside. It seems the rest of the worms have managed to escape and now wriggle around the lining of my jacket.

I baited my second rod, grabbed my net, and limped over to the willow tree. A single lady's shoe lodges in the crown. Lower branches reach out over a bed of bulrushes that hug the bank, providing protection to a moorhen and her three chicks. The rushes are on the verge of flowering. Though their stems look dry and brittle, their seed heads are soft and cottony like candy floss, and the gentle breeze scatters them over the pool's surface.

I stalked around until I found a spot where I could flick my float around the rushes, without tangling in the willow overhead. It was a small window, but I have fished for long enough to determine the force and angle required to get my bait safely where it's needed. The first cast landed short. I had overcompensated for the branches above my head. I lowered my rod for the second cast and whipped it horizontally with a little more vigour. The float landed with a satisfying plop at the edge of the rushes. I didn't bait the swim; I knew there would be fish there.

It was only minutes before the float began to tremble. The first time it bobbed, my heart skipped a beat. You must be patient with tench, and I managed to resist the urge to strike. It dipped a couple more times before disappearing violently beneath the surface. I struck, hard and low, making sure to avoid the branches above. The rod instantly jolted and curved into the weight of a fish. There is no greater feeling, and that moment has woken me from more dreams than I can remember. Thankfully the fish darted outwards to the centre of the pool, instead of coming towards me, into the rushes. I let the spool spill out as I manoeuvred my way from the willow. Once clear, I trapped the line with my finger and pumped the rod. The fish ran again in response, and I thought for a second I had hooked a carp. Following a couple more determined runs and a close encounter with the lily pads, the handle of my reel became easier to turn, and after ten minutes or so I lowered my net into the pool to scoop out a fine-looking tench. It was a good size, 4lb 3oz according to the scales, and a beautiful golden green. I removed the hook from its lip before grabbing the camera from my satchel and taking a couple of shots.

They are particularly slippery fish, so I lifted the tench from the net carefully before lowering it back into the pool. I held it gently beneath the surface for some time, giving it the chance to recover. At last it darted into the rushes, and I pulled my hands from the water. Three leeches had attached themselves to my skin and I flicked them off with disgust.

Tench were once regarded for their healing properties, earning themselves the nickname "doctor fish". They were applied to all manner of ailments and skin conditions, and I had considered holding it against the rash on my left hand. I have so far put off removing the thorn lodged there. Landing that tench was uncomfortable and it was time I addressed the problem. Although there are no fresh blood spots on the hanky, the inflammation has grown, extending down past my wrist, and upwards towards my knuckles. I have had numerous allergic reactions to cats, but none so violent.

Carefully I unwrapped the handkerchief, inhaling sharply when I saw beneath. The rash is some five inches in length. Its centre is hard and grey, its outer edges a deep, angry red. The thorn still protruded from the surface, so I set about removing it with my tweezers. At first I worried about it snapping, leaving the end embedded in my hand. The thorn turned out to be as tough as iron and before long I pinched it between the tweezers as tightly as possible. It was deeper into my hand than I thought. I pulled with greater and greater force, and the pallid skin around it stretched upwards. It looked like it should hurt, but the rash had numbed any pain. Eventually the skin burst open, and an acrid yellow puss oozed from the wound, leaving the back of my hand ashen and cracked, as if burned. I studied the thorn between the tips of the tweezers. It was long and curved, with a barb at the tip; it looked like an eyeless fish hook used to tie flies. I pulled the scotch from my satchel and poured a little into the sticky lesion. Feeling had returned and I gasped in pain. For good measure I took a swig from the bottle, before folding my hanky over to a clean section and tying it back round my hand.

Emma

Unless I continue to pull them out, I am usually a little subdued after returning my first fish. It was the same at Christmas when I was a boy. I always preferred Christmas Eve; the day itself couldn't possibly live up to the magical sense of anticipation that gilds the night before. So it is with fishing. I lower my first catch back into the pool and the excitement blurs away in the cloudy water before something like a hangover descends.

To ward this off I usually keep busy; I try a new swim, change up the rig, or swap out my bait. But the pain in my hand and ankle is making me tired. Instead, I pour out a decent scotch and sit here under the bivvy, writing up my catch. I look down at my jeans. They are caked again in thick black mud.

I said Emma made me choose between her and fishing. She didn't. She would never have done that. She didn't like me going as often as I did, but she never tried to stop me doing something I loved. Emma wanted children. It was me that stopped her. Like other parts of my life I find unpalatable, I managed to ignore the pain I was causing, until eventually it drove her away. I can't remember why I dragged my feet - laziness, selfishness, fear perhaps. None of these things would have mattered. Emma was good enough to make up for it. She would have made me better. She did make me better. I clung to her and drew from her and offered little in return. And now it's too late.

As I write these words, I realise how quiet it is. Not quiet, silent. Pools are naturally peaceful places, one of the reasons I love them so much, but rarely are they silent. The moorhen's song, the beat of water, the suthering of wind in the trees; pools will gently communicate with anyone who wants to listen. Right now, the world is paused. Time has stopped. There is nothing.

The moment is violently shattered by a barking dog. I exhale deeply, almost with relief; I must have been holding my breath. Another dog joins in and the ferocity of their snarls triggers some instinctive fear. They sound close by, on the lawn of the house. Maybe there were guard dogs after all. Water plays tricks with your ears, and I can't see them. The barking begins to fade, and I wonder if they are behind me, somewhere in the woods. They grow quieter and quieter. Now they are gone. I won't be satisfied until I've had a proper look.

I got up from the chair and let out a sharp cry. My left boot has become two sizes too small. I hobbled over to the pool to observe the full sweep of the lawn. A pale moon has emerged, and the westering sun has sunk towards the moors. The surface of the millpond shimmers, reflecting light back in all directions. Through this dazzling white veil, I saw a woman on the opposite bank. Though little more than a flickering silhouette, I could feel her watching me. We faced each other for several moments before she turned and ran up the sloping lawn. She beat her arms against her sides before soaring into the air and landing on the roof of the house a heron.

Mild visions are common by a pool. Anyone who has stared at a float in jabbly water will recognise the melting of the bank when they look down at their feet. But there is more as I write this. The rooks take flight in their dozens and circle the lawn shrieking. Impossibly they continue to rise from the ash trees. As they draw closer together, they go quiet, and there is no sound other than the beat of their wings against the air. This pulsing flock grows tighter and tighter until there is no sky left between them. I look up at this solid black square hanging silently over the pool and am stricken with a sudden terror. It is the darkest thing I have ever seen, absolute nothingness. Before the sight of it overwhelms me, it collapses again into birds, scattering noisily into different corners of the sky.

I smoke a cigarette and take a swig of scotch. It was a reflection surely, a reflection of the pool in the air around the birds. A moor grime slipped quietly down from the ridge behind the woods and this fine mist was just waiting for the sun to reach the right height before it echoed back the surface of the millpond, its brightness somehow inverted. That was it, a reflection. I am thankful for this journal. To write a thing down is to capture it. Once you have trapped it on the page you can analyse a thing, make sense of it.

It is time to get my first rod in again. Spending long periods in my own company requires the discipline of staying active. The carp are yet to rise so I will stick to ledgering. I am going to try a cat biscuit. Somerfield's own brand is the one variety that sinks without immediately breaking down in the water. They are too hard to put directly on the hook, so I'm going to tie a hair rig. That big fish must be somewhere. There is still a patch of water unruffled by the cross wind. I'm going to get my bait in there if it kills me.

A hare

Time flows differently through water and the last few hours have slipped quietly into the gloaming. The sunset was the most vivid I can remember, a long goodbye as we tip towards winter. With the last of the light ebbing behind the trees, the pool flooded with crimson.

I have yet to follow my tench up with a carp, or indeed anything at all. Time fishing is never time wasted though. I have fleshed my journal entries out with further detail, finished off the hard-boiled eggs, and watched the millpond settle in for the night.

After casting and recasting a number of times, that calm patch in front of the lily pads still eludes me. There is a science to fishing, no doubt, but a large part is instinct and hunch. I know if I can get my ledger to sink into that still square of water, I will hook a carp.

With the sun now sleeping, the intense heat of the day has seeped into the earth. As I pulled the tight neck of the gansey over my head, I heard the scratch of claws. I panicked a little, blinded by thick wool, and forced my head up and out too quickly, scraping flat my folded ears. A large hare bolted out from beneath the bivvy and stopped at the edge of the woods behind me. It stood up tall on its hind legs in that slightly unsettling way that makes hares appear human. Then it darted from sight, swallowed by the purple shadows thickening beneath the hawthorn. *I shall go intill a hare, With sorrow and sych and meikle care; And I shall go in the devil's name, Ay while I come home again.*

Other creatures emerge. A hob-owl lands on my tackle box, a giant moth with great brown eyes looking out through its wings. Faint rustlings creep from the woods - mice, foxes, maybe a badger. The midges are growing too and starting to bite. I light another cigarette and blow the smoke in looping trails around my head.

The moon is bright now, and a little past full. It is colder and whiter than the sun, but an effective source of light. The first star, the shepherd's lantern, attracts a pair of bats from the trees. They perform a twitchy dance above the pool's surface. Flittermice we used to call them. I follow one as it flickers from one space to another like a black strobe. Then it does something I've not seen before. It hangs in mid-air, pauses briefly and then shoots vertically upwards before dropping down again and landing at my feet with a slap.

I leaned forward in my chair to observe it. It observed me right back, its wings outstretched on the bank. I know bats are far from blind, but there was a curious intensity to its stare. I turned my head and it mirrored my movements, left and right, up and down. There was that smell too, like rotten meat.

Suddenly overwhelmed by a rush of anger, I kicked my foot at the thing. I expected it to leap out the way and take to the air. To my shame I made contact and sent it spinning into the pool. The water sucked it under with an unusual slurp. Guilt picked me up out the chair and over to the pool's edge.

There is nothing to see. Nothing at all. The water has darkened dramatically. It makes the pool look bottomless, like a hell kettle. It isn't just dark, it is black, so black it shines, like oil. Or an eye, a giant wet eye. I must be firm.

It is easy to get carried away night fishing. Sounds are emphasized, shadows exaggerated. Trees beautiful in daylight grow giant and menacing. *Ellum do grieve, Oak he do hate, Willow do walk, If you travels late.*

Fire will push back the night, create a wall between me and the darkness. I rip four blank pages from my journal, fold them over concertina-style and crumple them up. I place them in a small pyramid on the bank in front of me and build a tepee around it with six dry sticks gathered from the woods earlier. I tear out a fifth page, fold it and light one end before sliding it into the teepee's base. The paper catches quickly and before long the fire is alight. I slowly feed it with more sticks and relax into the crackle of wood, the dancing flames, and the sweet, intoxicating smell of smoke.

June 21, Saturday

The hunter

I must have drifted off. I am hiding beneath a bed. There is a broken mirror resting on the floor. In its reflection I am a girl, my face a mask of terror. I can hear the sound of heavy boots walking across the room. A giant hand thrusts into the darkness and grabs my wrist. I bite down on it as hard as I can. There is a terrible roar of pain and anger. It is so loud and animal-like it wakes me up, becoming the cry of an owl in the woods. *And owls shall dwell there and satyrs shall dance there.*

The dream still holds me, and I slide slowly into black water. I fight against the marsh, but with every effort to escape, I sink deeper. Flames flicker in front of me and the bank begins to emerge. The moon has risen in the sky. It shines down like a spotlight, tinting the millpond with a mercurial sheen. Stars fill the sky behind it, countless numbers floating through the darkness like a cloud of mayflies over the pool. The fire is dying so I feed it with a handful of small sticks and watch it burst back to life. I lean down into the flames to light a cigarette and wait for the nicotine to wake me up.

I reel in to find only a trace of cat biscuit left on my hook. Perhaps a carp has nibbled it down. I tell myself they are feeding at last; as a fisherman I am a creature of hope, and always willing to be deceived again. With renewed determination I cast at that spot by the lilies that has so far eluded me. It stands out because I cannot see it. Moonlight reflects off the pool, but that small patch is black, like a starless corner of the night sky. I cast a couple of times, but it lands one side or the other. On the third cast I try a different approach, ignoring my instincts and flicking my rod out to the left. The line arcs over the metallic water and looks a couple of metres off mark. At the last second, it cuts back to the right, as if caught by a sudden gust, and my ledger drops right in the middle of that dark square hole. I laugh out loud and place my rod on its two wooden rests, before pulling some slack off my reel and folding the foil over the hanging line.

As I write these words, I see the rash on my hand has grown again. It reaches my fingertips and is half way to my elbow. I'm going to have to unwrap the bandage and take another look. First, I'll treat myself to a nip of scotch and another cigarette.

I thought I had removed the thorn, but there was something protruding from the wound, a couple of millimetres flush from my skin. I gripped it with the tweezers and began to pull. I pulled and pulled, and still it kept coming. It was thin and strong, like fishing line. I pulled eighteen inches of it from my hand before I started to retch. Mercifully numbness returned, but the nausea overwhelmed me, and I dry retched again before it was out, all two feet of it. When I rolled it between my fingers it separated. It wasn't fishing line but a weave of some kind, like hair, grey wet hair. I tossed it onto the fire, and it hissed and curled, before catching light with a green, sulphurous flame. I leaned out the bivvy and threw up into the dark.

There was a flicker of light, and I was immediately alert. The line rose just enough for the foil to twitch. I wiped sick off my chin with the back of my hand and stood up quietly from the chair. It moved again. I held my right hand over the rod and my left hand beside the reel. I hold my breath. I wait. Time stops. The foil flies off the line and the reel starts to scream. I snatch the rod into the air and strike hard. The rod bends impossibly, and the reel screams again. I let it run. Somewhere in the distance a dog barks.

For fifteen minutes or so I just hung on. It tore across the pool, knocking me off balance as it turned abruptly in one direction and then another. Several times I was almost dragged into the water. It was like being pounded by some terrible storm. I applied pressure to keep it from the reeds and the lily pads, but it felt like the line or even the rod might snap. I hadn't set the resistance on my reel for something this heavy, so I couldn't effectively use the handle to stop it running. Instead, I pressed my middle and forefinger against the spool. Line continued to stream out, stripping skin from the surface of my fingertips. Mostly I let it dart, reeling in when the pressure eased. Eventually runs became shorter and less ferocious and after each one I wound in a little more line than I let out. Following some thirty minutes of this slow progress, it came to the top, halfway between the bank and the lily pads. It rolled over on the surface, its giant belly the reflection of the moon. It was enormous, I have never seen anything like it. I lowered my net into the water and it ran again. I let it go and secured the handle of my net beneath a tree root bursting up through the bank. I needed two hands on my rod to have any chance of landing the thing. At some point I brought it close again and it stayed near the top. It beat its tail fin on the surface with mighty slaps that echoed across the pool and sent waves crashing over the bank onto my boots. With one final run down and towards me, the line fell slack. I thought it had shed its hook. Then it appeared below me, like a ghost, and eased itself into the net. I threw my rod to the ground and with a roar of effort, dragged the netted creature up onto the bank.

I stood there, staring at it. It was a giant, the biggest carp I have ever caught, one of the biggest carp anyone has ever caught. It had to be 50lbs at least. It spilled out the net at both head and tail, and its great flank flashed silver and gold. Everything slowed as my brain drowned in endorphins. This was the moment I had been waiting for, that I had dreamed of since I was a boy.

After grabbing a score of shots with my camera I inspected the fish more closely and my elation started to fade. The carp's head and dorsal fin were a dull grey, like pencil lead. Along its flank was a grid of hexagonal red scales, creating a raised lattice pattern on its skin. Equally unusual was its forehead, which bulged forward over its eyes, almost a horn. It could have been a local peculiarity, or some atavistic gene. Except it wasn't similar. It was the same.

I should have ignored it, I should have enjoyed the moment, but I had to know. Carefully I lowered my hands between the fish and the bank, and with enormous strain heaved the leviathan over onto its other side. My heart tightened in my chest and my stomach hollowed. The distinctive pattern of red scales was repeated exactly, and carved into the centre of the fish's belly was a large circular scar, the bite mark of a giant lamprey. I staggered backwards and stared down at the thing. How could it be here? It was impossible.

Banked carp inhale and exhale heavily as they gasp for air. This one lay there calmly, smirking as it spat out the hook. Anger suddenly overwhelmed me, and I pulled a rod rest from the ground, gripping it like a stake. Surely I wasn't going to do this? I raised it over the beached fish and held it there, its sharp end pointing down. Emma would have stopped me. But she is not here. There is a deafening shriek from the ash trees and a huge cloud of rooks take to the air at once, a great dark shadow against the moon. I looked up at the flickering sky and the beast flipped smoothly over onto its other side. Before I could thrust the stick through its belly, it did it again and again, before finally dropping with an almighty splash into the pool.

I have never seen a carp half that weight move so effortlessly on the bank. I ignored this detail, there were too many other impossibilities to calculate without adding more. Tentatively I walked over to the pool's edge and looked down. There it was, a couple of yards out, its head twisted towards me, watching. It looked even bigger in water, at least four feet from lips to tail. At last it turned away and glided slowly through the pond, hugging the curve of the bank. I didn't want to, but I followed it, as if some force or other were making use of me against my will. I was pulled along behind the argent wake of that giant dorsal as it carved through the pool's surface. Without the satchel to force myself into the branches, I stopped at the hawthorn and breathed out in relief as the monster continued onwards. The skin tightened on my face. On the other side of the bush, just beyond view, there came the unmistakable sound of some giant creature dragging itself from the water. It flapped and splashed and gurgled with a terrible strangled choke, before slithering heavily and noisily into the woods behind. Then there was silence.

Blind eye

Writing this down starts me trembling, but I must get it on the page, expose it to the light. I pile more sticks on the fire. I must be careful what I write, I refuse to legitimise my fear with words. I sit here staring at the flickering ink and nothing else, nothing rational will take shape. I knock back three large slugs of whisky and light a cigarette. I must be firm; I must determine how to get back to the car.

Again, I am faced with a blank page. My ankle is not strong enough to get past the hawthorn, or the rhododendron in the other direction. Even if by some miracle I escape one of these obstacles, there's the sloping lawn, the drive, and a seven-foot gate to overcome. My only option is to go through the back of the estate, into the woods behind me. Yes, that's it, I will follow the path, wherever it leads, until I reach the other side.

Who am I fooling? Even the silhouettes before me are barely recognisable as trees. Beyond them is a dark wall. I lost my directions in daylight. If I try now, I will be benighted in moments. Besides, that's where it went.

I will not leave this place tonight. I must wait by the pool alone. I would do anything to be here with someone else, anyone. Not anyone; Emma. I had not let her go, not in my mind. I had trapped the ghost of her. It had been easy to forget I was alone until now. Now I look for her and she is gone.

I pulled the wind-up radio from my satchel and gave the handle a couple of shaky turns. It was tuned to Radio 4 and though the signal was poor, I could hear actors in some late-night play. I listened absently as I smoked a cigarette. After a short while I realised the broadcast was faulting and the same lines of dialogue were repeating over and over. I grabbed my pen and scribbled them down in my journal. There were several different voices, and their lines did not match. The transmission jumped and skipped like an old record.

"Take it!"

"But perhaps you are not altogether yourself."

"Stars. Hound. Tor. Coven."

The words were comforting at first, despite their lack of meaning. As they repeated themselves again and again, they lost the thing that made them reassuring, that made them human. They took on some other aspect altogether. It was their insistence, like they were growing in strength, like they were trying to come through. I flicked the radio off and there was silence, not the ghost of a sound. This was no better. So I am writing again. At least now I can hear some words, even if they are my own, and in my head.

Without warning I am suddenly afraid. My breath grows short and rapid before I know what is wrong. I look up from the journal and a cold terror clutches my heart. A light has come on in one of Rooksnest's upper windows, illuminating the lawn below. There is someone in there. The edge of the silence surrounding me begins to flicker. A faint melody carries on the breeze, the delicate sound of an old music box. Six notes repeat themselves over and over before stopping with an abrupt crash. The space it leaves is filled by a silhouette growing in the lighted room. It casts a shadow on the lawn that grows longer and longer, stopping only when it reaches the stone folly, and the giant figure of a man has filled the window. An appalling howl of despair carries into the night.

I shut my eyes to keep him out. There is cold water at my groin. Its foul stench fills my nostrils until I retch. I look up again and the window is no longer lit. It couldn't have been, it is bricked up behind the glass. It is the folly now that shines, burning red like a bonfire. The shadow of the flames stretches towards the pool. Moving now, over the water's surface, it drowns the reflection of the moon. It contracts and grows darker and slides onto the bank. It stops at the hawthorn and swallows it. The tree is a hole, a void, nothing.

Then there is something. I can't understand what I'm looking at. Long crooked fingers tear at the dirt as it drags its belly slowly along the moonlit bank. Its great gills swell outwards like billows with every gulp of air. A giant fin unfurls along its back, a spiky sail of bone and skin that it flicks against its rib cage with a wet slap. It looks up at me, its face partially obscured by coarse grey hair. One eye shines out from those moist folds of teeth and flesh, and I am overwhelmed by terror. Never have I seen such malevolence, such scorn and hatred. I can feel it as a physical thing, as vibrations through my skin. Its back legs kick out behind it redundantly, but it draws closer, set in cruel purpose.

I desperately want to stand from the chair, but my legs will not move. Some enormous force holds them in place. All I can do is write. No longer am I doing this to make sense of events or understand them in any way; I am well beyond the point of comprehension. No, now I write to try and bury these events in the past, to make the page a veil between myself and the unbearable present.

It stops, a metre or so along the bank, and rolls to one side, revealing a pattern of red scales and the large circular scar in its belly. A quivering arm reaches out towards me. It extends from its body to an impossible length with a series of dreadful cracks, before taking my left hand between its soft wet fingers. And with that the marsh floods out my dreams and I can feel myself sinking. I am being slowly, inevitably drawn into the earth, into the belly of the red cage. I cannot fight it. I must stop writing now. I must protect these words or there will be nothing left of me. I am sorry Emma. I was wrong.

Afterword by Jake Taylor

Uncle Pete's story ends there. With both curiosity and apprehension, I flicked through the rest of the journal. It is blank and water-damaged, with a handful of pages torn out. Only the last page has anything written on it, my uncle's scribbled directions from the Drab Tooth to the millpond. Attached to the inside of the back cover is an envelope with a small bundle inside. I pulled it out and placed it on the attic floor. On top was a Polaroid of Auntie Emma, laughing and pointing into the camera. Beneath this were four photographs of a good-size tench in a landing net. It is a beautiful golden green with fiery eyes and framed against a background of bulrushes. Underneath the photographs and folded into quarters, was an old clipping from *The Glossop Mail*, the conclusion to my uncle's tale.

Local man pulled from bog

Glossop resident Peter Taylor had a lucky escape when he was rescued from marshland outside the town of Chapelkill, near Whitby.

Peter was reported to be close to death and in a state of acute anxiety when the landlord of the town's Drab Tooth inn found him. He was chest deep in a bog that has claimed scores of cattle, deer and, allegedly, some unwitting ramblers.

It is reported Peter had been looking for Rooksnest Millpond. The pool was once a favourite spot for local fishermen, before it sunk into marshland following the town's great flood in 1977.

"Stugged for the night he was. No good will come of it." These were the words of the landlord who preferred not to be named. The landlord went on to say it took him and three local farmers more than two hours to pull Peter out.

The millpond had been part of the Rooksnest estate. The once attractive Georgian manor house is now derelict and partially collapsed where it borders onto the marsh that has overwhelmed the lawn and the pond behind it. Last serving as a council-run health facility, it closed permanently after the flood, and the death of its director.

Peter recovers in Whitby Community Hospital and is reportedly being treated for snail fever, a typically tropical disease caused by his prolonged exposure to the marsh's stagnant waters. Let's hope he gets well soon and can return home to Glossop.

The delicate state of Uncle Pete's mental health was probably why my dad had shielded me from him. Dad's generation doesn't deal with these things too well, choosing instead to cover them up and leave them unspoken. Still, it didn't quite add up. The detail and lucidity of my uncle's account seemed improbable in the face of such a dramatic breakdown. How had he continued to keep writing as the dark water swallowed him? I guess he could have committed it to his journal at any point afterwards. I'll never be able to ask him now, and that's going to nag away at me.

Dad called me down for lunch and we sat in the dusty kitchen eating sandwiches, not talking. Eventually he spoke, casually announcing the house was mine. It's what Uncle Pete would have wanted and that was the end of it. I didn't know what to say. I wanted to cry and hug my dad, but he didn't go in for that kind of thing. So I smiled and thanked him. That was that, my life was changed.
JT

BOOK TWO
THE HOUSE
(A confession)

Prologue

I almost missed it. It is a small article, several pages from the front. War dominates the news, and all other stories are getting lost in the horror.

"HIDE & SEEK TRAGEDY. Lily _____, 12, loses her life after second floor window fall. Police call circumstances surrounding the tragic death 'puzzling'. Locals from the nearby village of Chapelkill are said to be deeply saddened by this latest incident at Rooksnest Manor."

There it is, Rooksnest Manor. At last events have caught up with me.

One

He was never made welcome in Chapelkill. A mill owner from Manchester, Mr Woodlock moved his family across the Pennines at the behest of his wife, who hoped the cleaner air would improve the health of their sickly daughter. Locals would have accepted them, given time, but Mr Woodlock made errors of judgement that were not easy to forgive.

The role of squire was an important one in Chapelkill, carrying with it certain expectations. Mr Woodlock had slim regard for such matters and showed no interest in village customs or culture. He spent little time or money within the community and did not get involved in its politics unless it directly benefitted him. Mr Woodlock also brought his dogs with him, a pair of giant black Alsatians. They were too like wolves for the older villagers. The packs that had stalked the moorlands were kept alive by fireside tales; the young they had snatched and the livestock they had slaughtered not yet razed from memory. Others in the village called the dogs shucks or ratchets, though it was some time later before I understood what they meant by this. Mr Woodlock ran his house with a skeletal staff, and they did not speak kindly of him. It was with some trepidation I entered his employment.

Along with my classmates, I left the local school at the age of eleven. I had shown limited academic promise and my father naturally assumed that as his son and only child, I would one day take over the farm. My mother had more lofty plans for me. Through intractable determination and tireless hard work, my father had become a modestly successful sheep farmer and swineherd, managing to accrue enough surplus income for my mother to hire a governess. After spending the morning on the moors with my father, my afternoons were taken in the parlour under the tutelage of Miss Grimsditch. With half-rimmed spectacles balanced on the tip of her nose and thin silver hair swept up into an immaculate bun, Miss Grimsditch played the role of traditional spinster with considerable veracity. Indeed, her narrow piercing eyes and thin lips pressed into a permanent look of displeasure, betrayed little of her internal dialogue and would have made it easy to dismiss Miss Grimsditch as a caricature of her profession. But the scrutiny of a sheltered boy approaching manhood revealed a long slender neck and a ballerina's graceful poise; her large blue eyes were spellbinding, her skin impossibly smooth. In the tableaus of my imagination, she had been a not unattractive woman in her youth.

Beneath that immaculate skin, her story was a little more blemished. Miss Grimsditch was relieved of her previous post behind a curtain of whispers and rumour, a consequence, I have no doubt, of her unique interpretation of a suitable curriculum; for as well as teaching me algebra, Latin, biology and suchlike, my governess shared with me her more esoteric learning. Although she was a rationalist in every other way, time with Miss Grimsditch revealed her extensive understanding of the darker sciences. Her knowledge of the left-hand path was compendious. She taught me to grind down the shell of a boiled egg and prevent a hag from sailing it as a boat. I learnt how to identify a witch by hammering a tenpenny nail into her footprint. (For those ignorant of such matters, a witch is obliged to return to the spot and draw out the nail.) It was also Miss Grimsditch who told me the history of Rooksnest Manor and how the house had taken its name. I am getting ahead of myself. There is more I must tell you before we get to that.

Witchcraft had rooted itself in Miss Grimsditch's ancestry several centuries ago. With uncharacteristic pride and candour, she informed me of her descent from Roger

Nowell, the Justice of the Peace who had brought the trial against Lancashire's Old Demdike and the Pendle Coven. I never shared with my father Miss Grimsditch's parentage, or the hidden corners of her less conventional syllabus. On the one occasion I asked him whether he believed in witchcraft, my father was unusually short, dismissing my query as nonsense and forbidding me from making further enquiries; a reluctance to discuss the subject he shared with many others in the village. My father was looking for an excuse to call time on my education; the merest tincture of dark arts and I would have been dropped back on the moors with him, from sunup until sundown. This was becoming less and less the future I wanted for myself. I had come to relish my afternoons with Miss Grimsditch and the world beyond Chapelkill she had introduced me to. So I made a secret of my anomalous studies, a skill I was to become increasingly accomplished at.

Two

It was with gratitude to Miss Grimsditch I secured the position at Rooksnest. My governess spent her mornings at the house schooling Rose, Mr Woodlock's daughter, and became aware of her employer's intention to hire an apprentice to support him with the administration of his textile business. Miss Grimsditch could be an influential force when necessary and, like my mother, had a misplaced confidence in my abilities. At first my father balked at the idea and refused to relieve me of my responsibilities on the farm. After some gentle, and not so gentle persuasion from my mother, he eventually acquiesced.

The approach to the house was not a particularly pleasant one. The single lane track was long and sweeping and flanked on both sides by impenetrable thickets of rhododendron that threatened to overcome the property with a suffocating twist of branch and creature. Rooksnest itself was a fairly modest Georgian building lurking in the shadow of the moorland above. I had spent four prosaic years working on the top with my father, but from down there in its shadow the ridge took on a more sinister aspect. Irrational though it sounds, it was difficult to shake the feeling my presence had not gone unnoticed that first morning. A cloud of rooks swept over the house and landed along either side of the drive, observing me with dark scrutiny as I stepped cautiously between them. I was greeted at the door by Mrs Woodlock. She was strikingly beautiful, with raven hair, fiery eyes, and a distractingly female figure. It took no small degree of resolve not to gape at the sweeping curves emphasized with such effect by her fashionably tight-fitting dress.

Tea and pleasantries were dispensed before Mrs Woodlock's tone took a sharp turn and I was subjected to a barrage of personal questions. They probed a broad range of topics including spiritualism, politics, and women's rights. Looking back, she was evidently determining whether I would make a suitable companion for her daughter. At the time I had no idea what was happening and found the whole experience unsettling. It was the first of only three conversations I had with Mrs Woodlock and set the tone for all our exchanges thenceforth. Once satisfied I posed no immediate threat to Rose, Mrs Woodlock led me into her husband's study and the unfolding of this tale began.

Three

Mornings on the moorland with my father were supplanted by the scrutiny of ledgers in Mr Woodlock's study. As well as learning how to balance his accounts and draft new contracts, I got to accompany Mr Woodlock on visits to local suppliers, and the occasional excursion to his mill.

When I eventually proved my worth, Mr Woodlock provided me with a modest income. In those first few months, my employer paid instead for my schooling. This agreement suited Mr Woodlock as it gave him some control over my lessons and what I would need to learn to support him. Mr Woodlock was accomplished at getting his way. There was a force within him, a natural strength that he harnessed to drive through his agenda. Defined by his broad shoulders and enormous hands, Mr Woodlock was a giant of a man. With his large, neatly trimmed moustache and thick silver hair swept neatly back against his head, his demeanour was more in keeping with a hero in one of my adventure stories than with a northern mill owner.

What else is there to say about Mr Woodlock? He fished; I can confirm that. Should you ever find yourself in the Drab Tooth on the market place, ask if they still display the giant carp he dragged out the millpond behind Rooksnest. As for his inner life, my understanding of him is somewhat limited. Mr Woodlock was a man of few words and prone to extended periods of silence. Only during meetings with potential new clients did I catch a glimpse behind this veil. He was spellbinding to watch, bristling with charm and power as he hunted down a deal. I came to realise it was these moments he craved, not the financial rewards they brought with them.

Mr Woodlock's devotion to his wife was also self-evident. All our trips out involved the purchase of a trinket or other for Mrs Woodlock. At first this reverence seemed at odds with the ruthlessness with which he conducted his business affairs. I had seen him reduce grown men to tears with little effort and even less concern afterwards. The more time I spent with Mr Woodlock, the more I understood that his adoration for his wife was a natural consequence of his unquestioning self-belief. His sentiments towards his daughter, Rose, were somewhat more ambiguous. I am reluctant to jump to crass conclusions, but it was perhaps the case Mr Woodlock would have preferred a son. That, presumably, was the role assigned to me.

Whilst it wasn't obvious what Mr Woodlock thought of Rose, it was apparent to all that his wife doted on her, committing, as she did, her very soul to the care of their only child. It is testament to her tenacity that Mrs Woodlock persuaded her husband to move away from the cotton mill he loved, to give their ailing daughter a greater chance beyond the smoke and fog of Manchester. Mrs Woodlock was keen for her daughter to have contact with people her own age, so instead of being taught at home, I would spend my free afternoons schooled in the library at Rooksnest with Rose. Though weak and timid, and prone to visions and waking dreams, Rose's aptitude for learning was nothing short of brilliant. There were no disciplines in which she did not excel. It was through my determined efforts to try and keep pace with her that I grew beyond a merely average scholar.

Although not handsome in the conventional sense, Rose was completely captivating, like the painting of an angel, or a cathedral window saint. There was a light within her, as if her soul were glowing beneath the surface of her skin. I can admit without hyperbole that I quickly fell entirely in love with Rose. I had never met anyone of her kind. There were prettier girls in the village, but they were plucky and tough. They would tease me and make lewd comments when I passed them in the square. I now considered their behaviour vulgar and wholly inappropriate towards a young man of my new standing. Even Elizabeth's power over me was starting to wane. She had captivated me from behind the bar of the Drab Tooth for as long as I could remember Dad allowing me to join him there. Compared with Rose though, she barely registered in my affections. Rose was from some higher place. She used music, language, and art in ways I was unable to comprehend. I was only a summer younger than her, but I felt inferior to Rose in every way. She was ethereally beautiful, she was effortlessly accomplished at her studies, and she betrayed no feelings for me whatsoever. As frustrating as this was, it made me love her more. I worked hard at my lessons, I kept myself constantly updated with the debates of the day, and I served Mr Woodlock to the absolute best of my abilities. But as far as Rose was concerned, I did not exist.

With little experience of matters of the heart, I misread Rose's indifference as an arrogance, a calculated aloofness designed to belittle me. It was my own pride this conclusion revealed, not Rose's. Her detachment was not contrived for my benefit but was rooted in something more solid, the very walls of the house itself. Over time, Rose's pre-occupation with Rooksnest and its grounds grew into an obsession and a source of increasingly melodramatic distress.

Four

Although Rose's behaviour clearly frustrated Mr Woodlock, Miss Grimsditch nodded patiently to every story of phantom airships, creeping shadows, and disembodied whispers. During one of Rose's more outlandish tales, our governess caught a vague smile play at the corners of my mouth. As was increasingly the case, Rose retired back to her room after the account, worn out by its telling. Once we were alone Miss Grimsditch admonished me for my insensitivity and proceeded to recount some of the history of the house and the shameful events in the village's past that even then, so many years later, explained its residents' reticence to engage with certain subjects.

Miss Grimsditch had a gift for storytelling. She breathed a magic into her words, bringing events to life as if they were happening before you. As a child she had been privy to Roger Nowell's journals, their contents shared with her by her father, and by his father with him. The leather-bound books told of the Chapelkill Coven; a group of witches more infamous at the time than the one in Pendle. They had been wise-women, three generations of the same family, daughter, mother, grandmother. Villagers would visit them at their cottage in the woods. They came for advice, or good luck, or curing. But beliefs change, and communities are fickle and quick to judge. Stories of the women began to swirl. They were seen in congress with a man and his two black dogs. The stranger was long-haired and wore a cloak with an unusual breastpin. Accounts grew increasingly more outlandish, the women rode stags like horses, held wild sabbats amongst the old stones, and planted rings of exotic mushrooms to enchant the unwitting. Before long, all misfortunes were blamed on the family - the death of an infant, failure of the crop, any murrain infecting the livestock. When Roger Nowell became aware of the rumours, he planned a visit to Chapelkill. The opportunity was abruptly denied by the villagers themselves. They dispensed their own form of justice, swiftly and mercilessly one terrible midwinter night.

Beneath a fish-belly sky snow begins to fall. Vesper bells ring for evening prayer, but the pews in the chapel sit empty. The town's menfolk gather on the market place, armed with pitchforks and burning torches, roused by drink and the dramatic testimony of a child. They march on a cottage in the heart of the forest, fathers and husbands and sons. The accused are brutally beaten, their thumbs snapped, their foreheads sliced. They are dragged through the night, bloodied and senseless, their screams lost in the howling wind. This dark procession reaches the millpond at the woodland's edge. The women are ducked, again and again. With black water filling their lungs, they are hanged without trial or conference. Still twisting and writhing on the rope, their bodies are set ablaze. Green flames light up the sky, and the ungodly screaming echoed until dawn. Rotting flesh hung on the air, beyond the New Year, beyond the next year, lingering on through times of ill fate. The gallows trees still pierce the earth, for they are the ash that grow on the lawn by the millpond, their roots as deep as their canopies tall. The rooks came on Christmas Eve to pick the bones apart. And they stayed.

Five

As I have already confessed, I felt wholly inferior to Rose. At one time I would have accepted this without reflection, but due to my new sense of status, I could no longer brook Rose's effortless disdain. The one advantage I could claim was her sensitivity. This was her weak point, the wound in which I would twist the knife. Despite repeated assurances to Miss Grimsditch I would do no such thing, I recounted to Rose the town's dark history.

From that day onwards Rose grew more withdrawn, more prone to waking visions, night terrors and somnambulism. One winter night the housemaid found her in the gardens at the back of the house. She was standing beneath the ash trees looking up, threading severed strands of her hair through the bark. After that her bedroom door was locked from the outside. I regretted what I had done, but to my further shame, I was more afraid of being exposed as the catalyst for Rose's steepening descent into malady.

Rose's increasingly erratic behaviour was a mounting source of resentment for Mr Woodlock who became less and less tolerant of her episodes. As his relationship with his daughter began to fray, so too did that with his wife. It is against this background of sharpening tension I recall my instructions to collect a parcel from the market. *Dr Wistman's Golden Spindles* had sold antiques and curios from a stall beside the well for longer than anyone could remember.

The carriage dropped me off outside the library. It was a crisp March morning and the sun shone with that occasional brilliance of early spring, rendering the market with a vividness that solicited a heightened response from my faculties. This clarity made the following events stranger still. Screaming bled through first, piercing, corvid shrieks. The stalls and the light melted away and I was suddenly alone beneath the moon, watching with detachment as three figures danced widdershins around the well. It was just as Miss Grimsditch had described the child's testimony that drove the village to murder. The three women were stripped from the waist up, throwing back their heads and leaping upwards to impossible heights in increasingly frantic gyres. I noticed Dr Wistman watching me, and the bustling market painted back round. A sneer slipped from the stallkeeper's pale upper lip, and he beckoned me over with a curled finger. I can remember little of the subsequent exchange.

Six

It was unusual for Mr Woodlock to interrupt our lessons. He looked uncomfortable as he hovered at the doorway, stiffly holding out the box I had collected from Dr Wistman the previous morning. Rose did not notice him and continued to read from the Yeats collection Miss Grimsditch had set. Although our tutor had clearly acknowledged the appearance of her employer, she did not stop Rose, and bristled visibly at Mr Woodlock's presence. After several long seconds of awkward shuffling, Mr Woodlock marched into the room and placed the gift on the desk before us.

"We are in the middle of our studies Mr Woodlock. It is to her detriment you cut Rose short."

"I'll be the judge of what is to the detriment of my daughter thank-you Miss Grimsditch."

"But perhaps you are not altogether yourself." Mr Woodlock's face flushed crimson and his knuckles paled as he gripped the edges of the box.

"You are relieved for the day Miss Grimsditch."

"I'm afraid that's not possible. Rose needs me."

"As I said Miss Grimsditch you are relieved for the day. I am quite happy to extend your leave for the rest of the week, or for the month or indeed indefinitely should you wish. I am led to believe such an abrupt conclusion to your role as governess would not be one you are unfamiliar with."

Miss Grimsditch rose with quiet dignity, gathered her paperwork, and slipped it into a case. Before she stood up to leave, she squeezed Rose's hand and whispered something into her ear.

Although my account of the events at Rooksnest is largely without dialogue, I think it useful to present this exchange with as much detail as my recollection permits, for it is the only understanding I have of the relationship between Mr Woodlock and Miss Grimsditch. Somewhere in those words was a clue, a signpost as to the direction events might turn. Alas, I didn't see it then and even now I struggle to comprehend everything that occurred from that moment forwards. Sometimes at night the conversation comes back to me. I am in the library, seated in the armchair by the fire and reading from an old book. In that uncertain passage between sleep and waking, I understand everything that happened at Rooksnest, for it is written there on the pages in front of me. I awake with a jolt of terror and shame. To my relief the epiphany fades as I open my eyes, my conscious mind grateful to its counterpart for swallowing that terrible truth and threading it once more through the fictional scenery of nightmares.

After Miss Grimsditch's departure, the room was absolutely still. Rose remained seated, the book of poems open in her hands. Mr Woodlock stood behind her, motionless. I stared at the parcel on the desk around which we were frozen like figures in an ambiguous mezzotint. Eventually Mr Woodlock broke the silence.

      "Open the box Rose. It is for you."

Rose did not react. Silence reasserted itself, finally broken with sudden violence by my employer. He moved with unnerving speed, his large hands tearing through the card like a predator stripping the flesh of its prey. The box was swiftly destroyed revealing the gift inside, an ornate musical carousel.

The carousel was expensively and expertly crafted. Beneath the hexagonal red crown of the canopy was a woodland scene, through which six stags galloped in pursuit of a monstrous boar. Upon the back of each stag sat a small girl, their faces ceramic, their frightened expressions rendered with an unnerving accuracy.

Turning away from the toy at last, I noticed a tremble in Rose's hands. She stared at the carousel, her eyes wide. Ignorant of his daughter's discomfort, Mr Woodlock opened the top. It revealed a key, which slowly and deliberately he began to turn. Rose's shaking grew more acute, the spine of her book tapping against the table like the insistent knock on a door of one hellbent on entry. The key turned and the mechanism tightened, and Rose's head began to sway. I made to interrupt him, but Mr Woodlock stared me down with such fury I turned away in fear. It was then I noticed the red spot spreading across Rose's book. I looked up and watched with alarm the droplets of blood drip from her nose. Mr Woodlock let go of the key and the carousel burst into life. From somewhere behind its clockwork teeth, a music box began to chime, an eerie unknown melody to which the six stags charged through the woods, the girls clinging to their backs as if for their lives. Rose began to scream.

Although it could likely be rationalised as an involuntary physical response to the sudden shattering of that unbearable tension, I have no doubt something else burst forth and knocked me from the chair. By the time I had scrambled to my feet, Rose was fleeing from the room. Mr Woodlock stood with his back to me, watching her leave. When he turned around, I recoiled in fear. Again, you will no doubt explain this away as a reaction to the shock, but I stand by what I saw. It wasn't Mr Woodlock's face that looked down on me but Dr Wistman's sneering grin. The image was fleeting, and Mr Woodlock quickly returned, mercifully dismissing me for the remains of the day.

Seven

I never discussed the episode in the library. As far as I am aware, the words on this page are the first time events have been told in their entirety. It is likely Miss Grimsditch gathered fragments of the tale from Rose, but not the complete story, as she gently pushed me on occasion to fill in the blanks. The fear of admitting some kind of mental schism, or of the incident affecting my employment with Mr Woodlock, was so great that despite a desperate yearning to share with someone what I had felt and seen that afternoon, I buried the events deep down, beyond the reach of Miss Grimsditch's subtle but compelling probing.

It was of no surprise Rose's disposition continued to deteriorate. What was of note was the change that manifested itself in our tutor. As well as covering the carousel with a shawl and moving our studies to the other end of the library, there was a distinct shift in Miss Grimsditch's overall bearing. Gone was the façade of measured calm and patience that had characterised her thus far. In its place was not quite anxiety but an alertness, a heightened response to the everyday sounds and movements we filter out as background noise.

Furthermore, Miss Grimsditch had taken to wearing a new piece of jewellery, an enormous silver locket in the shape of a heart, not a lover's heart, but an anatomically accurate heart, complete with arteries and ventricles and pulmonary veins. I watched her play with this macabre charm as Rose read aloud, fingering it nervously and turning it over and over until the chain on which it hung grew tight around her neck, cutting into her throat and flushing her pale skin crimson.

It was late one morning in the weeks that followed that the next significant event in the unfolding of this tale took place. I remember the house was unusually quiet. Miss Grimsditch had not yet arrived to begin preparation for our lessons and Mrs Woodlock was down in the village collecting a parcel from the post office. Rose's poor health had prompted the growth of her mother's interest in herbal remedies, and she had begun to order all manner of salves and lotions from across the globe. As was now usual, Rose had not come down from her bedroom and Mr Woodlock and I were in his study, drawing up a lucrative contract to supply new khaki service dress to the regiments of North Yorkshire, in anticipation of the impending conflict in Europe. The sound of breaking glass abruptly shattered the peace, followed by an unearthly shriek. Mr Woodlock sighed wearily and put down his pen.

"Wait here."

I remained at the desk as instructed and watched Mr Woodlock stride impatiently from the room. A crisp copy of *The Times* newspaper was folded over the blotter pad. One column had been circled with a pen. Unwilling to move the newspaper, I scanned the short article, upside-down. Written by astronomer Clarence Chant, it documented a great meteor procession observed in the skies over Canada and America, and as far south as Brazil. Witnesses described a parade of some fifty slow-moving fireballs moving between the horizons in an identical path, accompanied by thunder, and the trembling of the ground. It was a fascinating account, but I began to grow restless. Along with the library next door, the study was the oldest part of Rooksnest. The two rooms had been adapted from some existing building and the rest of the house built around them. I had grown accustomed to the library, but I did not like being alone in Mr Woodlock's study. It felt cut off from the rest of Rooksnest, stranded almost.

I got up to stretch my legs. The study was both opulent and pared back. Everything was hewn from meticulously polished wood, the panelled walls, the grandfather clock, the great oak desk, and the drinks cabinet beside the two leather armchairs in which Mr Woodlock entertained clients. There were no ornaments or paintings; the only decoration was an antique fishing rod mounted in a case above the fire. Books were limited to a single shelf on the wall behind Mr Woodlock's desk, a small, functional assemblage of dictionaries, maps, and biographies. I understand the collection in the library next door had come with the house when Mr Woodlock purchased it and am sure my employer had no knowledge of its contents. I moved over to the only interesting feature in the room, a telescope standing by the window and looking up into the sky. Elaborately attached to a metal tripod, it was an intimidating-looking apparatus, more like a weapon than a scientific instrument. Mr Woodlock had acquired it only recently after developing a sudden uncharacteristic interest in stargazing. I lowered my head towards the eyepiece when the sound of Rose's wailing suddenly burst into the study. I was reluctant to ignore a direct command from my employer, but it was such a discordant noise that a fearful curiosity got the better of me. I crept quietly across the room and poked my head gingerly out the door. The study was off the hallway leading up to the foot of the staircase. From my position I could make out Rose on the top step clutching a straw doll like a child. Mr Woodlock stood on the step below. Although I could not distinguish his choice of words, Mr Woodlock's body language made it clear he was not happy with Rose for her interruption of our work. Rose appeared oblivious, as if in a trance, and continued to wail. Suddenly she noticed something from the corner of her eye and turned her head. With a look I do not wish to remember, she pointed to something at the bottom of the stairs and began to scream.

Seemingly without thinking, Mr Woodlock struck Rose, once. As I have said, he was a large and powerful man. I don't believe he was always aware of his strength, especially in the throes of an uncharacteristic loss of control. Mr Woodlock knocked his daughter clean off her feet and down the great staircase. Rose's body crumpled from one step to the next in terrible, spasmodic jerks, her appalling descent recalling the dance of an unskilfully manipulated marionette. Without thinking I ducked back into the study, waited a moment, and came running out as if I had just heard the commotion. Mr Woodlock charged down the stairs.

"Sleepwalking. She has fallen. She was sleepwalking!"

Eight

Rose was blighted by the most severe fevers, headaches, joint pain, and insomnia. She did not respond well to the circus of doctors, healers and pharmacists Mrs Woodlock procured to treat her. They prescribed a variety of different medicines and regimes, but Roses' condition only worsened. For several weeks, her chances were considered hopeless, and the reverend began to make regular, sombre visits to the house. It was his wife who diagnosed a sleeping sickness and provided Rose with a course of dried mushrooms. Days later, Mrs Woodlock found her daughter sat up in bed reading. Although stabilised and showing gradual signs of improvement, Rose was all but bedridden for the rest of my time at Rooksnest, and I saw her again on only two more occasions.

I am certain Mr Woodlock never told his wife the truth of what happened that morning on the staircase. One afternoon shortly after, Mrs Woodlock made an unexpected visit to the library. Mr Woodlock was spending more and more time away from the house and was that day attending to some unspecified matters at the mill. Miss Grimsditch did not look surprised to see Mrs Woodlock and instructed me to put down my books. For the next forty-five minutes I was interrogated about Rose's fall. Mrs Woodlock asked me the same questions again and again. *What had I seen? What had I heard? What was Mr Woodlock's response?* And every time I told the same story - I knew nothing about the incident except Rose had screamed and Mr Woodlock had rushed from the room to care for her.

It is with deep shame and regret I recall these events, buried as they've been until now. Part of my duplicity was straightforward cowardice. Mr Woodlock was a giant of a man with intimidating physical strength. Barely seventeen years old at the time, I did not possess the resolve to challenge him. More shameful than this was my pride. I had grown accustomed to the elevated status I had acquired in the village and the modest wages I was being paid. Men whom I had looked up to all my short life now nodded to me in the street and shopkeepers served me with a newfound respect and favour. I was after all, the squire's right-hand man. Despite Mr Woodlock's unpopularity, old traditions die hard, and he was held with grudging, but nonetheless not inconsiderable esteem. I did not want to tell anyone what Mr Woodlock had done because I knew that would be the end of my apprenticeship, and the end of my chance to escape a future on the farm.

With ill health confining Rose to her room, Mrs Woodlock's interest in natural remedies mutated into obsession. Ordering tinctures and treatments from the world's leading healers and apothecarists was not precipitating the pace of change in her daughter Mrs Woodlock sought, and so with a now encyclopaedic knowledge of the subject, she resolved to build a walled garden and cultivate herbs and fungi of her own. Mrs Woodlock consulted a series of titles borrowed from the local library before drafting her sketches, plans that required the felling of the estate's ash trees. The garden had recently been invaded by strangleweed, broomrape and witch's hair. To root them out, the groundskeeper had started to clear some of the rhododendron, revealing an antiquarian arrangement of stones. This discovery had unsettled Rooksnest's staff, and the groundskeeper was reluctant to undertake further landscaping. After continued pressing on the matter from Mrs Woodlock, he abruptly left her employment. Mrs Woodlock approached a number of local gardeners and labourers, but to her frustration none within the village would accept the task. Even with enquiries made further afield, Mrs Woodlock could find nobody within the county to take up the contract. It was around this time events began to gather pace.

Nine

My nights had become plagued by the most vivid and diabolical visions. No matter how abstract and nonsensical these dreams were, they consistently featured the same three characters, Rose, Mrs Woodlock and Miss Grimsditch. Whilst their faces were familiar, their behaviour was anything but; their language was coarse or spoken in tongues, their conduct lewd to the point of bestial. In each ritual I was the focus of this dark and vulgar attention. Though their deportment was beyond the realms of anything I had witnessed whilst waking, it felt real, as if I were peering into a hidden part of their marrow, a part that manifested only when they came together, when they were three. This union made them strong, more than human, more than I could resist, their power filling me with equal parts ecstasy and disgust.

Following a fortnight of fitful slumber, I lay awake one night in the darkness, the wind's howls twisting the house in which I had grown up into something unfamiliar. Some panel or other must have worked itself loose on the roof. It plagued the chimney breast in my bedroom with an incessant rattling, banging, and scratching, as if something were desperate to get in. Out of frustration more than need, I pulled a coat over my shoulders and marched down the stairs to relieve myself in the courtyard lavatory.

I knew the house well enough to dispense with a candle. As I turned into the kitchen at the foot of the stairs, my senses were immediately troubled, and I regretted my haste. Born and raised there on the edge of the moors, I was accustomed to the absolute darkness of night, but the blackness before me was less an absence of light, and more a thing of form. I would have turned around and crept back up to bed were it not for the pressure that had built abruptly and uncomfortably beneath my belly, elevating the journey to one of necessity. I plunged forward, stumbling against something hard piled up on the kitchen floor. In a combination of both surprise and pain I called out. Instead of air exiting my mouth, something rushed in, choking my cry, and filling my throat like smoke. I coughed and staggered across the kitchen. Fumbling desperately with bolts and locks, I could feel the darkness massing behind me, gently pushing me against the door. With suffocating panic, I at last managed to drag it open and stagger out into the night. I could not bear the pain in my bladder another second and relieved myself in the middle of the moonlit courtyard. To my horror, it wasn't liquid I ejected, but a pale cloud of tiny spores. It burned and itched as it seeped out of me and drifted upwards into the dark sky.

I awoke with a jolt in the comfort and warmth of my own bed, the coat still wrapped around my shoulders. My parents never made mention of the incident, so I came to conclude the events had occurred within the confines of my mind. I discounted evidence to the contrary, the angry welt on my shin and the unlocked kitchen door, and although my recollection of the incident yielded the oppressive dread of previous nightmares, it did not demonstrate the usual mercy of transience.

Ten

The following afternoon found me at my books as usual. Miss Grimsditch was now dividing her time between me and Rose. At the start of our lessons, she would assess and correct my work from the previous day, before setting me a new task and retiring upstairs to Rose's bedroom for the remainder of our studies. Forbidden from joining them, I worked alone in the library. This was by no means an inconvenience. I hadn't seen Rose since her fall and considered meeting her with a mixture of guilt and revulsion.

The library had always felt too large for the house. From the adjoining rooms it was difficult to picture how the available space could accommodate its dimensions. I usually managed to overlook this anomaly, but on that day, there was a distinct sensation of oppressiveness in there, claustrophobia almost, as if the room could no longer afford its own contents.

The book shelves ran from floor to ceiling and occupied most of the three walls on which they were mounted. In the middle of the room were further stacks arranged in diagonal lines to match the repeating pattern in the parquet floor. At intervals between the stacks were a series of wooden desks at which I took it in turns to study each afternoon. My favourite desk was by the doors onto the lawn, not for the extra light this afforded but because of the cloven circular scorch mark seared into the mahogany beside the ink well. Unsurprisingly my governess had a fantastic explanation for its existence. In the middle of the nineteenth century, spiritualism came to possess the upper classes. During a séance held by a previous owner of the house, the visiting medium managed to conjure Lucifer himself through the black shadow of his scrying glass. He appeared briefly on the desk in a burst of flaming brimstone before he was banished back to hell. I always suspected Miss Grimsditch was trying to frighten me in punishment for some of the inconsiderate responses I had shown Rose's sensitivity, but my tutor assured me she was telling the truth. One morning she dug out an ancient volume from the library shelves describing a similar incident at an ecclesiastical college in Manchester. It had an unusual smell, and its animal skin cover was sealed shut by two tarnished metal clasps. I thanked my governess, but when she left the room, I stashed the title beneath a pile of books that turned up one day on the table beside the fireplace.

Unable to concentrate on my work that afternoon, I considered whether this was the day to read the account Miss Grimsditch had earmarked. As I approached the fireplace, I was slowed by a curious trepidation. The logs in the grate were stacked higher than usual and sat there unlit, despite autumn's growing chill. I knew them to be deadfall from the ash trees; Miss Grimsditch insisted on it. For centuries ash has been burnt on the hearth to ward off the malevolent. Staring at that tangle of wood and bark, it became apparent something was amiss; there was a kind of liquidity to it, a shifting and squirming. The previous night's terrors suddenly descended, and the fireplace burst apart in a cloud of grey spores that rushed up the chimney as smoke. The scene hadn't finished with me yet and drew me inexorably towards it. No longer acting under my own volition, I dropped to the floor and worked my hand into the firing. With my arm buried almost to the elbow, my fingers found a thing that had no place there. Concealed inside the hard cold wood was something soft and warm, and wet to the touch. I pushed in my finger and damp meat closed around it, the toothless gums of some suckling creature. The sensation repulsed me, but I was unable to withdraw my arm. To my horror, I squeezed the fleshy thing into my fist and tore it from the darkness. As I pulled my hand from the fireplace, I could feel something else against the skin, cold and metallic. I wasn't surprised when I uncurled my fingers. Though it was blackened with soot, I knew immediately what I was clutching - the heart of a bull shot through with nails. Thanks to the more unorthodox aspects of the education provided by Miss Grimsditch, I knew the heart was a charm, protection against the attack of dark magic.

Though unsurprised to find such an object, I was taken aback by my subsequent reaction. In sudden anger, I threw the heart with all my vigour against the wall. It clung to the wooden panelling for a time before sliding slowly down and landing with a gentle slap on the floor. I stamped on it again and again with all the fury I could summon. With the charm obliterated, the grip of the dream loosened, and I felt something withdraw from the room. As quickly as it slipped away, I was beset by guilt and panic for my lack of self-control and the sticky crimson mess at my feet.

Eleven

It was soon, perhaps days after I discovered the heart in the fireplace, that the following episode occurred. I was studying in the library when Rose began to scream. It is difficult to adequately convey the singularity of that sound. It brought to mind the rage of a moorland storm or the deafening roar of the mill floor at full production. Although I had become desensitized to the afflictions of Rose's condition, there was something so animal-like in that cry it acted immediately on my nerves.

Miss Grimsditch had expressly forbidden me from visiting Rose's room so I could justify my inaction, but fear held me back, not loyalty to my tutor. The idea of facing whatever Rose was experiencing rooted me to the spot, rendering me incapable of movement.

The screaming continued and became accompanied by the thud and crash of toppling furniture. The urgency of these sounds triggered something in a buried layer of my brain and adrenalin overcame the immobility of fear, dragging me up onto my feet and out the library.

As I made my way along the hallway Rose's screams grew more distressing, as if the innermost part of her soul were being scraped out. It seemed a physical impression applied directly to my brain rather than through the receptors of my faculties. I ran, not through any notion of heroic duty, but because I knew if I delayed, my resolve would falter, and I would turn around and flee.

When I burst through the door into Rose's bedroom, nothing in my short history could have prepared me for the sight that greeted me. Rose was tied to the bed, her arms and legs secured to the posts with knotted sheets. She screamed and writhed, the force of her efforts twisting her features into a mask of bestial hate. Miss Grimsditch stood beside the nightstand chanting the same words over and over, *I abjure thee and summon thee forth from this girl!* I felt the detachment of a dream as I looked around. The window was open and a gale blew through the room; I watched it pluck the mirror from the wall and send it smashing to the floor. The furniture was shaking, hopping, banging, and daubed on the wall, in what I can only guess from the colour to have been a mixture of blood and excrement, were the words, *Rook, rook get out of my sight, or else I'll eat thy liver and thy light.*

I watched Miss Grimsditch remove a short cane from her bag. It had a silver bulbed-handle and a black iron tip. With sudden violence she struck it against the soles of Rose's feet. She did it again and again and again. Rose's scream changed from one of fury to one of pain and at last I found the strength to move, leaping across the room and grabbing my tutor by the wrist. *Let me go, you don't understand!* But now that I had acted, I was resolute, and dragged Miss Grimsditch away from the bed. Just as suddenly everything stopped. The window slammed shut, the furniture was immobilised, and Rose screamed no more. The room fell silent. Instantly the pressure on my heart was relieved and the atmosphere resumed its normal condition.

I let go of Miss Grimsditch and untied Rose's limbs. The mask of fury on her face had gone. In its place was the muddled aspect of the somnambulist, woken in the moonlight outside their bedroom door. With her arms freed, Rose sat up and grabbed her feet. *You don't understand,* repeated Miss Grimsditch, the last words she would ever speak to me.

Twelve

I recounted everything I witnessed that day, and everything I knew about Miss Grimsditch to the Woodlocks and again to the authorities. Although each of my interrogators assured me I was doing the right thing, and that it was my responsibility to give as much information as possible, I knew this was the final betrayal. I tried hard to avoid discovering what happened to Miss Grimsditch, but it is difficult to hide from gossip in a small community. It appeared she was spared a jail sentence but was admitted to an institution for observation and testing.

In the days that followed I finished off the work Miss Grimsditch had set. When I wasn't studying in the library, I found myself inclined by some compelling force to search the house. It was during these investigations I unearthed a number of artefacts concealed around the estate. I removed a pair of open scissors hidden beneath the mat outside the library's exterior door. Behind the plant pot on the steps up to the front of the house I discovered three clay figures, clumsy likenesses of the Woodlocks. On a shelf in the library, concealed behind a row of encyclopaedias, was my most macabre discovery, a witch bottle - a glass flask filled with urine, nail clippings and hair, all of which, I have no doubt, taken from Rose's person. I had seen images of all these items before in my studies. They were charms, protection against attack from witchcraft. I took them to my employer. Mr Woodlock still raged against Miss Grimsditch, for the nature of her teaching, for what he considered the torture of his daughter, and for the introduction of superstition and the irrational into his house. He smashed the charms beneath his large boots and cast them into the fire.

With the artefacts destroyed, my compulsion to search the house faded and some semblance of calm returned to Rooksnest. Rose was all but bedridden, Mr Woodlock found more and more reasons to be away at the mill, and Mrs Woodlock busied herself with plans for the medicine garden. Against this background of relative normality, I recall that final afternoon in the house. The clarity of events flicker in my memory, sometimes returning with merciless clarity, other times drifting through my dreams with a welcome vagueness. But I can never completely forget. The thick circular scar on the back of my hand has itched without relief since that day, a constant nagging reminder of what I saw.

Thirteen

Whilst the Woodlocks searched for a new governess, I found anything to occupy my time, anything to avoid working with my father on the moors. I'm ashamed typing these words, but this is the truth of it. I was in the library reading a book about lichens when I noticed Mrs Woodlock marching determinedly across the lawn towards the woodshed. Moments later she struggled back again, dragging with her a long-handled felling axe. I put down my books to help her, or perhaps deter her, I can no longer recall. Before I could open the glass doors leading onto the garden, I noticed a distinctive melody creeping through the silent house. Despite having heard it only once before, that haunting hexatonic scale was lodged in my mind, and I knew instantly it was the sound of the carousel trickling down from Rose's bedroom. With that realisation I left the library and made way up the staircase, my self-control ebbing away with every note.

Although conscious of an aversion to entering Rose's bedroom, I could no longer claim ownership of my will. I pushed open the door and stepped inside. On the nightstand beside the small iron bed, the carousel spun furiously. I stared at it, transfixed. Even through the blur of their ordeal, the faces of the six girls riding the galloping stags conveyed a degree of terror imperceptible when the toy was at a standstill. When at last I looked away, I noticed Rose stood by the window gazing out across the lawn, her head gently bobbing from side to side. I called out to her. Beyond my mouth my voice slowed down and stretched out, squeezed thin by the air. When her name eventually broke through this thickening body of vapours, Rose's head stopped still before turning slowly towards me. Although her body remained stationary, her head wound further and further round, until it was twisted into an impossible angle, the muscles and sinews in her neck straining, threatening any moment to tear through the skin. To my further horror it wasn't Rose's face that crept menacingly into view, but that of an old woman, her ancient skin pale and cracked. The corners of her mouth rose into a smile of such utter menace, I heard myself moaning with fear. I watched, terror clutching my heart, as her neck straightened out like a corkscrew, realigning the upper and lower parts of her body. With that her face became her own again and Rose opened her arms as if to embrace me. Despite my fear, or maybe because of it, I desperately wanted to hold her, to feel her against me. I took a step forward. Only then did I notice the space between her feet and the floorboards. She was hovering, rising and falling gently with her breath. Her expression flickered like a guttering candle, oscillating between a desperate plea for help and a terrible mask of hatred. When she opened her mouth as if to scream it stretched wider and wider, until it was impossibly wide and she began to vomit, long grey hair, thick like a horse's tail.

A scream from the back of the house broke the spell. Looking past Rose and through the window, I saw Mrs Woodlock on the lawn below, desperately flailing her arms. Above her head, rooks, hideously taloned, dropped from the sky and attacked her with increasing fury. Wave after wave of the black birds rose from the spinney of ash trees until the garden spun with dark feathers.

With a sudden return of my faculties, I turned and ran from Rose's bedroom and downstairs into the library. The glass doors onto the lawn were stuck in their frame and I struggled desperately to pull them open. Outside the shriek of rooks was deafening. They continued to rise from the ash trees in their scores, scraping away the sky with flickering black scratches. They circled the millpond in ever decreasing gyres before diving in threes, tearing at Mrs Woodlock with gruesome hooks.

When at last I wrenched open the doors, the smell of rotting flesh burned my senses. I ran forward across the lawn but was knocked to the ground before I knew I was being attacked. The foul stench and the piercing shrieks had driven Mr Woodlock's Alsatians into a frenzy, and one had jumped at me from behind, knocking me to the ground. By the time I got to my feet the dog had backed off, positioning itself between me and Mrs Woodlock. It crouched before me snarling, its back end raised, its head and front legs flat against the lawn. I took a step towards it, towards Mrs Woodlock, and it started to shake its head, those powerful jaws snapping open and shut. From the corner of my eye, I saw something moving at pace. I turned to face Mr Woodlock's other Alsatian charging across the lawn towards me. I awaited its approach with a degree of calmness, almost of disinterest. Beyond a certain threshold the brain applies its own anaesthetic, and a merciful condition of stupefaction descends. The dog leapt at me from an unlikely distance and once more I was face down in the dirt. This time I was unable to stand up straight. The great beast had gripped my hand in its mouth and was shaking its head, stripping skin from bone. Whilst the itch of that scar has never been adequately scratched, there is more than mere discomfort as I write this. I can feel the pressure once again of those dreadful jaws, the terrible fear my thumb will not withstand, that it will burst in a bloody cloud of cartilage and splintered bone.

Although certain moments are seared into my memories, the chronology of events and how they link together is somewhat blurred. At some point the dog let go of my hand and took up sentry between myself and Mrs Woodlock. Blood poured from the wound. I tried to stand but had become weak and sunk back down to my knees. I found myself in the centre of a faerie ring, a circle of red mushrooms pushing their way up through the grass. Across the lawn, in the light of the pale sun, the old stones glowed like burning coals.

Above my head a change was manifesting itself in the rooks that filled the air. It is hard to convey what I saw, but it was as if they were smoothing out, losing that thing which distinguished them as individual birds, losing their "rookness" if you will. They were becoming black spots in the sky, points of absolute nothingness, an absence of matter. I watched in horror as they twisted closer and closer together until they were impossibly close, and they weren't separate things any more. No longer was there wing and beak and claw, there was only darkness, a perfect square of nothing. It hung in the air above the lawn, an unfinished section of painting, or a patch of midnight in the afternoon. I remember vividly my terror upon realising I was close to an unknowable force that could crush me easily as I could crush an insect. I looked into that dark horror and could feel it judging me, dismissing me for what I was. An irrelevance.

Free at last from the onslaught of rooks, Mrs Woodlock ran back towards the house, towards me. A crimson drape of blood obscured her face. Beneath it much of the skin had been sheared away. Her nose and lips had gone leaving dull grey holes into her skull.

The dogs were in a rage, desperate for the kill, but she ran towards them regardless. I too ignored their foaming, snapping jaws and held out my arms, willing Mrs Woodlock forward. She never made it. I watched, impotent, as the dark shape dropped from the sky and swallowed her, disappearing her from sight. And with that the black square collapsed once more into a flock of birds and returned silently to the ash trees. A period of absolute stillness followed into which Mrs Woodlock's body materialised, hanging in mid-air as if by some invisible cord. As soon as my brain acknowledged this anomalous vision, Mrs Woodlock dropped from the sky and plummeted into the millpond, striking the surface without a splash. I believe by that point I had journeyed to the very edges of terror and revulsion beyond which no man can return without forever losing his sanity. It was the crack of gunshot that stemmed the permanent splintering of my mind. By the second shot both dogs were down in a pool of their own blood.

Mr Woodlock threw the shotgun to the ground and raced across the lawn towards me. I raised an arm towards the millpond, and he changed direction, before plunging headlong into the dark water. Moments later he staggered up the muddy bank, his wife's lifeless body in his arms. Even from that distance I could see her features were unmarked. There was no blood or wounds, and her clothes, though sodden, were undamaged. This is the last thing I remember.

Epilogue

Until now I have never provided a full account of what happened at Rooksnest. I am adept at keeping things to myself, spinning half-truths, even telling outright lies. Mrs Woodlock's body was unmarked. What was there to gain by my tale of malevolent birds and floating voids? I had no wish to accompany Miss Grimsditch to the sanatorium. So I left unchallenged the police's verdict that Mrs Woodlock had drowned, driven into the millpond by her own dogs.

I never returned to Rooksnest. Following my attack by his Alsatians, Mr Woodlock provided a private hospital in Whitby with enough funds for me to recover at leisure. I managed to avoid the war. As part of my psychological therapy, I offered the doctor just enough of my version of events for him to declare me unsuitable for conscription, but not enough to keep me at the hospital against my will. I was encouraged to open up, to tell my story - I should not feel guilty it saved me from the trenches. Yet I do. I knew what I was doing. My life has been a series of disguised betrayals and self-justified acts of cowardice. Whilst you might struggle to provide evidence I am in any way evil, were you to connect the dots of my experience and behaviours, you would be left with a picture of moral ambivalence at best.

And so my life continued. Whilst I was enjoying the hospitality provided by Mr Woodlock, one of his associates visited me. I call him an associate for my sake; rival would be a more accurate description. He owned Foggbrook Mill near Glossop, a market town on the western edge of the Pennines. He came to Whitby on the train to offer me a job, keen to exploit my extensive book of contacts. I knew I should feel ashamed of my disloyalty to my employer, but Mr Woodlock had made it easier for me. He had not deemed to visit me once during my recuperation, so I could look down on my guilt from some sense of moral high ground. As I said, I had become more comfortable with betrayal than any good man should be. By this time

Mr Woodlock's own business was collapsing. He failed to fulfil the uniform order placed by the North Yorkshire regiments and, with my help, my new employer secured the rest of the contract.

As the cotton trade died, I moved from one struggling mill to another, before finally settling at a firm of accountants in Stockport. I am not blessed with a wife or children and have always been the right-hand man, lacking the drive or courage to establish a business of my own. But I have been comfortable and safe, more than I have the right to ask for.

And then like an atavistic gene, the past has burst its way to the surface once more. Brief though it is, the newspaper article describing Lily's fall to her death is enough for me to draw the parallel. For that it is exactly how it happened over twenty-five years previously.

The rest of this account takes place during my convalescence in Whitby. It was almost Christmas when Rose fell from her bedroom window and snapped her neck on the lawn below. Something inside me was still broken at that time and I greeted the news of her death with virtual indifference. The police investigation considered somnambulism but remained inconclusive. Fresh muddy bootprints on the floor of Rose's room matched none of the treads on her father's shoes, but their unusually large size was enough for the village to reach a judgement.

There were further pieces of evidence, a series of random strike marks on the floorboards beneath Rose's bed, and an ugly bite mark on the back of his hand Mr Woodlock was unable to account for. Following the death of his family, my former employer signed up to the local regiment and was shipped off to Flanders, never returning from the cold death of the trenches.

If I had told my story earlier, could I have saved Lily? Could I have averted a death reduced to forty words in a newspaper already filled with horror? Perhaps. Yet still I do nothing. If you are reading this, I am already dead. What is it but a confession to my own judges, an attempt to assuage my guilt?

I should ask myself how many more people will lose their lives in that house. I should ask myself that. But instead I will bury the question, conceal the truth of it. And they will grow stronger, as they always have, until they push their way back through.

BOOK THREE
THE STONES
(A midwinter horror)

PART ONE
THE LIBRARY

"Though we meticulously measure and chart our landscape, the landscape is itself a map, of something we have all of us endeavoured to forget."
The Plateaus of the White Peak, Doctor Alfred Wistman

Reading Room

I will tell you everything I can remember.

I was approaching the conclusion of a PHD in biology. To help fund my studies I spent free afternoons and weekends working at the Northcliffe Library. This left little time to return home to Marple. Dad was quite ill by then and had been moved into a nursing home. My brother and my mum lived nearby and kept me updated. It was important I finished my research.

The Northcliffe is a magical place, a dark cathedral of books, maps, and manuscripts glowering with gothic defiance between Manchester's shining glass boxes. Gargoyles protect its columns and parapets, spitting rainwater onto intruders below. Its giant doorway looms over Deansgate, ornate and imposing, like the fortified gatehouse of a castle. Inside the library, the tangle of pillars and vaulting is cut from Cumbrian Shawk. Follow the sunlight along the winding corridors and the stone shifts from a cold grey to a fleshy pink, stirring in you the not wholly unpleasant sensation you are sliding into the belly of a living thing.

The library's nave is its magnificent Reading Room, gently lit by stained glass and clerestory windows. Standing guard over the wooden alcoves that flank the sides of this cavernous chamber are statues of history's great scientists and philosophers. Miles of shelving stratify the walls, climbing up through the floor of the mezzanine above. Like a woodland canopy folding over the stars, the most impressive of the library's vaulted ceilings hangs high overhead. Stone constellations divide the sky - comets, toadstools, and wild boars, in a network of delicate bosses.

Working in the Reading Room was a continuous privilege. It sits three storeys above street level, elevated to muffle the "skeletal clatter" of the Victorian coaches below. After closing time, I would sometimes hear echoes of those carriages rattling slowly over the fog-drenched cobbles. There is an amplified silence in the Reading Room at night. It is almost a physical thing, stretching the space between books until shadows of other moments slip through.

As for the collection itself, it includes all the milestones of printing, lavishly illustrated and exquisitely bound. The library boasts a copy of the Gutenberg Bible, a first edition of Shakespeare's sonnets, and original fragments from the *Epic of Gilgamesh*. It assembles an exhaustive range of disciplines – history, theology, exploration, philosophy, science, and the arts. It is Manchester's memory of itself and the world, gathered, restored, and catalogued into a meaningful whole. You will find a million stories in the Northcliffe, but not the one you are about to read. This tale was told to me in part by William Kearney, the library's most senior archivist. The rest of the story is my own.

The Pennine Institute of Geology

It was thanks to William I secured my job at the Northcliffe. I had studied in there as an undergraduate and we struck up a sort of friendship. It was William who told me about the vacancy and coaxed me through the application process. Once I started in post, it was with William I shared most of my shifts.

Though we spent many hours working side by side, I can tell you little about William. Even his appearance is difficult to reassemble from my memories. The one thing I can confirm with any certainty is the circular scar on the back of his hand, a little like a bite mark, the result of a particularly severe and untreated case of ringworm. William offered nothing of his personal life and expected nothing in return. This arrangement suited me. I am the product of reading rather than experience, and talking about myself does not come easily.

William began his account one afternoon as we catalogued a crate of recently acquired medical texts. I had taken the unusual step of telling him about Dad's illness. Our mutual discomfort at my disclosure of this personal information hung over the room like a thick smoke and one of us had to clear the air.

William's voice was thin and cracked. I understood he suffered from an infection of the lungs. His capillaries were choked by a living fur, grown from the invisible spores he had inhaled hunched over the library's ancient books. I had to listen carefully when he spoke, blocking out any extraneous sounds. In spite of his condition, William was an accomplished storyteller. So carefully did he build his words around a tale, it lived in your memories like one of your own.

William's story concerned Alfred Wistman, a Doctor of Philosophy at the Pennine Institute of Geology. Established in the nineteenth century by wealthy industrialists from Manchester, Oldham and Stockport, the Institute was wound up in the 1950s and its mission and aims are now difficult to trace. There are few mentions of it in geological journals. References that do exist dismiss it as a curio, a vanity project for the rich millowners who funded it. The Institute's idyllic location on the banks of the Woodhead Reservoir perhaps substantiates this allegation.

I was familiar with William's description of the spot. By the time I was a boy the Institute was little more than a bite mark in the ground, with sections of collapsed wall thrusting obliquely through the earth like broken teeth. Dad took my brother Tom and me up there every week, one long glorious summer. Work had unusually granted him leave for our entire school holidays, and he used that time to teach me to swim in the reservoir. Despite being younger than me, Tom was already confident in the water by then and took great delight in proving it. I remember

Dad's unwavering patience and kindness, despite my stubborn fear and ineptitude. Then one day I pushed off from the wooden jetty and paddled out alone. I can see his face, beaming with pride and joy, as I swim back into his open arms.

Gallant soldier

According to William's account, Alfred Wistman's reputation as a geologist began to grow in 1920, after his return from the horror of the trenches. He had served as a rifleman in the 33rd Division and spent most of the war dug into a ridge somewhere east of Ypres. In October 1917, his entire infantry was cut down in the battle of Polygon Wood. Months of shelling decimated this ancient and beautiful forest. The land turned inside out and upside down; it was as close to hell on earth as you could imagine.

They found Alfred's shattered body folded into the trunk of a hollow tree. Soldiers carried him by stretcher to the Vampyr Dugout, a sprawling underground headquarters near Zonnebeke. The British Tunnelling Company had excavated a hospital, mess room, chapel, kitchen, workshop, and dormitory, joined into a hexagon by a network of tunnels. Railway irons and wooden beams supported its chambers, built to withstand fifty feet of rocks and clay, and the relentless German shelling, a sanctuary beneath the slaughter and destruction above.

It seemed refuge had come too late for Alfred. They covered his broken frame and laid it out on the chapel floor, guts spilling from his belly. For two days he was left alone with the dead, a crooked line of dark shadows leaking onto the cold stone. As the nurse sponged the blood and dirt from Alfred's neck in preparation for his burial, she jolted in shock. Alfred had gripped her by the wrist. Then he opened his eyes and began to scream.

Alfred's journey back from the threshold was swift and celebrated in the dugout as a miracle amidst the endless misery and suffering. He spent the remainder of the war recovering in a Belgian field hospital. Influenza withered those around him, but Alfred grew stronger and returned to England a hero. The Pennine Institute heard his story and provided a grant for him to study at the Manchester Albert University. He became a scholar of sedimentology and developed a personal interest in a number of other topics including comets and standing stones.

I am getting ahead of myself. This is information gathered from my own investigations and did not form part of William's tale. During what should have been the final months of my doctorate, I devoted more and more study time to tracing, reading, and annotating Alfred's work.

Devil's-bit scabious

William's story picked up again after Alfred's completion of his PHD, whereupon he became Doctor Wistman and joined the Pennine Institute as a researcher. His studies considered the interplay between geology and ecology, and he spent much of his time on the moors collecting lichens. A lichen is a symbiont, a fungus and an alga; the fungus protects the alga from their environment, and the alga provides the fungus with food. This fascinated Dr Wistman, and his ground-breaking work would pioneer the development of lichenometry. By 1930 he was in demand as a guest lecturer at universities on both sides of the Pennines.

During those early years Dr Wistman was a familiar figure around Manchester's educational institutions, striding across their quadrangles in his Tielocken, the long khaki trench coat marked by the mud and blood of the battlefield. But the war never let go of Alfred and refused him any comfort from his newfound status. Academic life and the responsibility of his standing slowly ate away at him, and he spent an increasing amount of time seeking solace at Chetham's, Manchester's other great library.

Some of the books in Chetham's have sat on the shelf since 1653. The building itself is older still, built to accommodate a college of priests from the adjoining church, now Manchester Cathedral. At the end of the sixteenth century Queen Elizabeth awarded wardenship of the college to her advisor – astronomer, mathematician and magician, Doctor John Dee.

According to William, it was one of the librarians at Chetham's who first introduced Alfred to Dee. The two doctors worked from the same table in the Audit Room, some 340 years apart. Scorched into one corner of that ancient oak desk is a hoof-shaped burn, a memory of the profane practices that had seen Dee charged with sorcery and driven from the capital. With apparent earnestness, William described how this burn marks the spot where Dee summoned a demon with the ancient magic of his scrying glass. As Dee banished the screaming beast back into the underworld, it burned with the fires of hell, scorching into the wood a permanent memory of that diabolical rite.

Though he was a rationalist in every other way, this story had a profound effect on Dr Wistman, who spent more and more of his time tracking down Dee's work. He became obsessed with one particular title, *Mercurius Coelestis*, an apocryphal text, the existence of which William doubted. Wistman's fascination with Dee directed his work down darker paths, paths science has long since forsaken. William did not expand on this, for it was here he abruptly reached the end of his account.

Reindeer moss
As the pressure of my PHD mounted, I spent an increasing amount of time at the Northcliffe. William's account of Dr Wistman had got under my skin. I felt sure he was keeping something from me. Despite its connection with the university and its reputation as a

research hub, there is little reference to the work of Dr Wistman in the library. What entries do exist mention him in passing or are heavily redacted. In 1950 they stop abruptly, as if he simply disappeared. Before long, I spent all my study time chasing phantom shelf references and speculatively ordering uncatalogued items from offsite archives.

There were practical reasons for my consuming interest in Dr Wistman. Clear symmetries existed between our research, and I could not understand why I hadn't come across his work before. My own dissertation considered parasitism and questioned the symbiotic relationship within lichens. It proposed that the fungus is not protecting the alga at all, but is trapping it, endlessly dragging out its natural life so it could continue to feed. Though Alfred and I disagreed on this, I was as fascinated by the organism as he was. There was something else that drew me to him though, something more personal.

It was lonely watching Dad's decline. I had no partner and everyone I had previously called a friend had drifted away with work, or a relationship, or a new social circle. The university found me accommodation in Fallowfield, but I shared little in common with my housemates. They insisted people who study science do so because they lack imagination. At first I cared enough to challenge their perceptions. I remember joining them at the Friendship Inn one night and sermonising about my studies. My housemates did not share this enthusiasm for lichen and immediately changed the subject. Upon returning from work the following evening, I found a note on the kitchen table, *"We've gone for a drink. See you when we get home."*

I guess I saw a kindred spirit in Dr Wistman. I let him into my mind like a cuckoo's egg and allowed him to grow there without noticing. His papers continued to elude me, and I wasted more and more time pursuing false leads and dead ends. I was convinced things were being kept hidden, that there was a story there yearning to be told. Dad's memory was failing by this point and on the few occasions I visited him he struggled to recall who I was, or who he had been. I should have helped him remember. Instead, I devoted my time to finding someone else.

A large golden bee

It was William who brought me the rest of the story. I was studying an effigy of the Green Man carved into the entrance to the Reading Room. His stone face was drawn with hawthorn leaves, curling out from his nose and eyes. Fanged teeth and a fixed stare conveyed menace, but also a kindness. This ambiguous intention was captivating, and I visibly jumped when a loud knocking echoed down the library's stone corridors. I recovered to find William locking the door to the restricted archive. Though I had never been in there, I knew it to house the collection's older and more valuable texts. A glimpse revealed itself as he pulled the door shut. It looked like another smaller library in there, with wood panelling and a parquet floor. I wondered then if there was another, even smaller library beyond that. And another beyond that. Perhaps they went on forever.

William held a yellowing envelope of microfiche sheets, which he tapped nervously against his leg. After solemnly describing the envelope's contents, he pointedly refused to hand it over. During the impasse that followed, William expressed his regret for introducing me to Dr Wistman's work. I lied, insisting Alfred's journals were essential to the completion of my dissertation and without them I would likely fail the course. Eventually William acquiesced.

The envelope was dusty and torn. There were six sheets of film inside, along with the flattened, dead skin of a spider. My hands trembled as I powered up the reader. I have always been fascinated by the process, all that information shrunk so small as to encrypt it. Reading any document from a microfiche is to discover a secret, and always prickles me with excitement.

Although by no means a complete account of his studies, those films were a wealth of information on Dr Wistman's work and filled in the detail missing from William's tale. I embarked on my research by studying Alfred's portrait. It was a colour photograph, torn in two. With one half missing, there was little in the way of context, but Alfred looked to be a tall thin man, somewhere in his fifties. He cut a rather awkward, stooped figure, as if uncomfortable in his body. This is unkind, he was, after all, living with the scars of war. Alfred's hair was straight and grey, and unusually long for a man of that time. It partly hung over his eyes, which were sunk into a spare, almost skeletal face. His skin was pale, particularly above the mouth, as if his upper lip had never recovered from the shaving of a long-worn moustache. Alfred sported his famed Tielocken. There was no sign of military insignia on his coat, but attached to the left of his buttons, just above his heart, was an unusual-looking breastpin. It was a large golden bee, the length of a man's middle finger. Dr Wistman stood with his foot resting on a small red crate, revealing the pattern inside his trench coat. With a little digging I discovered the coat was an early design for British officers, its lining eschewing the tailor's trademark check for a bold hexagonal print.

Calcination

The bulk of the content in the microfiche collection was from a journal entitled *The Plateaus of the White Peak*. Beginning as a conventional field study, it is filled with beautiful pencil drawings of synclines, rock outcrops and wildflowers, accompanied by comprehensive and exquisitely calligraphed notes. Alfred's interest in lichens continues, which he evidences with impassioned descriptions of the species.

"Lichens are pioneers. They were the first to escape the sea, mapping the contours of our rocky outcrop in black and orange and silver bands. When new land is violently torn up by volcanoes, or scoured blank by glaciers, it is lichens that bring change. They draw the marrow from the rock, re-purposing its minerals so that other organisms may emerge. Lichen is deemed a parasite, but it is so much more. It is truly transformative, taking inanimate matter and creating life."

The journal was enthralling, and I could not understand why it was kept from the public. After several months of entries however, its contents abruptly change. Alfred's interest in John Dee happens suddenly and completely, and his records become an enthused account of the Doctor's research.

"Dee was a keen antiquarian and one of the first scholars to postulate the existence and power of ley lines. His interest was cultivated by the London Stone. Originally found on Candlewick Street, facing the door to St Swithin's, the Stone is believed to be London's most ancient monument. Some suggest it is 3,000 years old, brought to London after the fall of Troy. In 'Jerusalem', Blake paints the Stone as an altar upon which Druids performed their bloody ritual, whilst others maintain it was part of an older circle, or a marker at the intersection of powerful leys.

Whatever the Stone's true history, Dee was convinced of its thaumaturgic properties. He believed such sites record an echo of the human experience they have witnessed - sexual rites, blood sacrifice, dancing, music, prayer. The rock holds it all, layer over layer, and amplifies it at times of astronomical significance. Behind nightfall, to avoid the gaze of those who would have him tried for sorcery, Dee stole through the city's quieted streets. Under cover of darkness, he chipped away at the London Stone, collecting its shards for application in his alchemical transmutations."

Around this time, I finally went to see Dad. I knew he would be keen to hear about Dr Wistman and his interest in the megalithic. Dad's memories were held in stone. Get him onto anything antiquarian and he found a hidden path through his darkening history, joining things together that had drifted apart. I liked talking with Dad about our past. It was easy to overlook his illness. He could recall things I had forgotten, describing distant events with precise detail. On this occasion Dad was distracted and disinterested in my account. He interrupted me frequently, complaining about his dinner and how his stuff was going missing. His stories were muddled, jumping from one episode to the next like the narrative of a dream. Before long he became trapped in a loop, a litany of fractured images repeating itself over and over. Only a handful of words made it through this tumble of syllables – *stars, hound, tor, coven.*

Dad had been a physicist all his life and could find patterns in the incomprehensible. Although I had taken for granted the clarity of his thinking, the simplicity with which he could explain the most complex idea, it was a characteristic I respected greatly and one of the reasons I chose to study science. But as I sat there in his room, I grew increasingly impatient, angry even, angry with him for being ill.

Dad and I were alike, everyone said so. I could not bear to see him like that; I could not bear to see myself like that. As Dad began to change, so too did I. I existed partly inside his memories of me. As those memories faltered, they took my story with them and buried it in the entropy of his collapsing mind. I wanted to remember Dad as he was when I was a boy – the strongest, cleverest, and kindest man there was. The shadow of his condition threatened to cast itself backwards and obscure my childhood. So I let the space between us grow. Despite pleas from Mum and Tom, I provided one excuse after another not to return.

I suppressed my guilt at how I was treating Dad, but I did not escape it. It transformed into something physical, a persistent itch between my toes that I scratched until the skin became raw and blistered. It was not only Dad I began to treat with contempt. I abandoned any attempt to endear myself to my housemates. Their lives were vulgar distractions - drinking and one-night stands and pretentious art shows. I was doing a thing of worth, of real meaning. My research into Dr Wistman connected me with something important. I wasn't filling time like they were, I was nurturing a thing, helping it grow. There was an excitement in my blood I had never felt. For those few weeks I was more alive than ever before.

Stonecrop

Dr Wistman's visits to the White Peak continued, though he replaced his study of its geology and related ecology with the extensive cataloguing of antiquarian sites. He returned again and again to Stanton Moor, a gritstone upland between Bakewell and Matlock. Here he drew and mapped with meticulous detail Stanton's myriad of ancient features – erratics, cairns, and standing stones.

Alfred's accounts of Stanton were enthralling, and I felt compelled to visit the moorland myself. It would give me something to talk about with Dad when I found the time to see him. My father's obsession with the archaic ensured our holidays and days out always incorporated a trip to an earthworks, or menhir, or henge of some kind. I remember fondly our trip to Spinster's Rock in Devon. The Rock is a dolmen, three vertical stones supporting an enormous sixteen-ton capstone roof above. It is said that a coven of witches cast it together in a single morning. Local folklore provides a warning to the curious - circle the stones six times widdershins and a giant toad will emerge, before dragging you into the ground. Dad dismissed these stories. He believed the name spinster derived from a Celtic word meaning "open to the stars".

After the Rock collapsed in the nineteenth century, local villagers rebuilt it. This fascinated Tom and I, and we dared each other to lie between the three uprights. As I write this I am there again. It is not only images that return but the smell of damp rock, the response of leaves to the wind. I feel the same tingle of joy and terror gazing up through cold shadows to that giant capstone obscuring the sky. Our challenge ends in stalemate when two large hands grab our wrists and drag us into the light. *I don't want to explain to Mum you've been pressed liked wildflowers.*

Please forgive my digressions. The chronology of events is blurring a little at the edges, and there is still much I need to tell you.

I approached Stanton Moor through the village of Birchover. From this aspect it is difficult to appreciate your elevated position. Only when you reach the Eastern edge of the upland does the ground drop sharply away and reveal spectacular views over the Derwent Valley below. I watched a man pointing distant features out to his son, and a vague recollection of standing there with my own father tried to materialise.

I wandered the moorland clutching a map drawn from Dr Wistman's journal. Thick purple heather obscures some of the sights he listed, but the Nine Ladies is still plain. It is a small Bronze Age circle, some four thousand years old, attracting hundreds of druids and pagans on the solstice. The Church appropriated its story, claiming the stones were nine girls, petrified by an angry God for dancing on the Sabbath. Meandering slowly through the surrounding trees, I marvelled at the tributes decorating their branches – talismans, wooden hearts, and twig frames woven with ribbon and wool. Hidden in the twist of their roots were poems and photographs and prayers.

I dropped down onto my knees to study the clumps of liberty caps marking the woodland borders. They pushed up through the wet grass, tiny reflections of the stones they circled. As I held one gently between my fingers, the suspicion I was being watched suddenly latched onto my breathing. I spun around. A hooded figure sunk into the tangle of rhododendron. It was a fleeting vision. With my focus corrected I saw in its place a lop-sided sign falling from the ground. It spelt out its warning in unambiguous terms – *No Digging Here.*

The Red Stag

The heather on Stanton's uplands flowers late in August and attracts clouds of bees when the nectar has dried up in the valleys below. Dr Wistman describes how he was collecting leaf samples and rock sediments amidst the low drone of the swarm, when he spied two men further down and to his west, hacking through a glacier of undergrowth. Alfred pulled his field glasses from their case and watched in awe as six standing stones slowly emerged from the earth. From his position on the ridge above, he could see their shape, a small, flattened hexagon.

In spite of an increasing social anxiety, Alfred could not contain his curiosity. After gathering his tools and sample jars in his knapsack, he strode down the escarpment. The two men were CJ Hawthorne and his son, local archaeologists eager to share with Alfred the history of their discovery, the small but ancient stone circle known as Doll Tor. Before the setting sun plunged the moor into darkness, the three men left the site and made their way down to Birchover, where Dr Wistman insisted the Hawthornes celebrate at the Red Stag Inn.

"Mr Hawthorne and his son toasted their singular discovery on the Moor as rightly they should. I insisted on purchasing the drinks in exchange for their unrivalled knowledge of local sites and features that might be of interest to the antiquarian. For every shot of whisky they gratefully requested, I returned from the bar with two, as they lived close by, in the village itself, and I could not risk their presence at the circle that night to protect their excavation. Nursing the same pint of beer all evening, I excused myself from drinking for fear of the horrors it conjured in me following the war, not altogether an untruth.

When the landlady rang the bell a final time, I helped Mr Hawthorne and his son to the door, and they drifted into the night with much merriment. My journey was shorter, for I had booked a room at the inn. After thanking our host, I retreated upstairs to check the contents of my knapsack. I was never without a hammer and chisel and was not short of sample jars. The one thing lacking was a good quality torch. During my frequent visits to the bar that evening, I had spied a suitable-looking device, hanging beside the cellar trapdoor. I just had to bide my time.

The harvest moon was large and bright. When the clouds broke, it bathed the moorland in pale light, exacerbating my impatience. I waited, pacing back and forth in front of the window. I removed the large golden bee from the lapel of my coat and turned it over and over in my hand, its touch against the skin curiously soothing. The day I purchased that ornamental pin is still clear to me. Although my life before the war is someone else's, his memories no longer my own, certain moments cling stubbornly on. Like that bee. I bought it for her from a stall on Chapelkill Market. Before she was taken by the black water. Before we were taken. Of course I remember the stallkeeper, tall and ashen and stooped. 'Wistman' was the name on his sign, the name I took when they dragged me out the darkness at Polygon Wood."

It seemed I was chasing a phantom. The man I had pursued these last few months was not even real. This revelation served only to excite my interest further. That he had come back from the war someone else, that there was another man to find, afforded me a strange, selfish thrill.

Alfred had chosen to be a ghost. Dad was not so fortunate. His past was being stolen from him, his memories buried in the earth. I could have helped him find them. Instead I tried to bring someone else back to life, someone with no valid claim on the present.

Doll Tor

"Satisfied the landlady was in her bed and asleep, I hoisted the knapsack onto my back before slipping from the room and creeping carefully along the landing. With the order of the creaking steps committed to memory, I clambered over them as quietly as my stiffened leg would permit. In the darkness of the snug at the bottom I felt along with my fingers for the bar hatch, before lifting it open and grabbing the torch from the hook beside the cellar trapdoor.

Beyond the bar was a small, gated courtyard. I stopped there for a time and questioned the ethicalness of my intention. But it is too late to pretend I am someone else. Experiences leading to this point already denied me the right to judge my actions through any moral lens. Besides, this was science, and I was on the edge of something. There is no doubt Dee would have justified the undertaking without a second thought. I buttoned my trench coat to the collar and slipped out into the night.

When the moon crept from behind the clouds I switched the torch off, unsure how long its batteries would provide. As I climbed the road out of Birchover, the light paled and much of my path faded into gloom. It planted inside me the unsettling notion I was stepping into the void. This fear was as much practical as it was esoteric; the moorland had been quarried for thousands of years, scraped out by a network of abandoned shafts and scars that would have plunged me to my death in an instant.

Held by darkness, the moorland was another place altogether. Moonlight illuminated the valley below, and it was indeed a wonderful sight; but somewhere in my delight of that achromic beauty there crept an unwelcome sense of unease, almost of dread. Wind cut through the heather in low soughs, and the impression the hill were breathing threatened to be formed and accepted. My admiration for the endeavour of our ancestors was replaced by a vague fear of that which they had been trying to appease. Huge dark rocks jutted from the landscape and challenged me to pass them. Quickly and completely, the irrational deference of former worshippers enveloped me, and I could not dispel the lingering image of these great black shadows crushing the human form in an appalling cloud of cartilage and splintered bone. That blood had been spilled on this ground was now an inexorable truth. I fancied that I could smell it, taste it, feel it squelch beneath my boots.

After lighting a Capstan to steady the nerves, I strode on until I found myself on the ridge above Doll Tor. The suspicion I was being observed grew as I looked down into the darkness. Eventually the feeling overwhelmed my reason and I span round. In the eye of the moon, the rocks appeared to have moved closer and encircled me, waking in me the strange and unwelcome sentiment I had strayed upon the borders of another world, a world where I was a trespasser, where my presence had been noted with hostility.

I almost fled back to the Red Stag at that moment, the pull of a locked door, a warm bed, and a glowing fire almost too great to resist. Am I not a man of science? Have I not learned to control my fear of shadows and the unknown? I look up to the heavens, to Orion's belt of stars, and from the hunter's strength I draw my own.

Before this resolve had a chance to crumble, I scrambled down the side of the moorland and into the trees surrounding Doll Tor. Upon reaching the circle I got straight to work, taking no time to absorb the atmosphere of the place for fear of losing my nerve. I removed my knapsack and quickly unpacked its contents. Upon positioning the flashlight to illuminate the stone before me, I inserted the sharpened tip of the chisel blade into a carving of rings making a flower. I took a breath. I lined the hammer up with the top of the chisel's handle and closed my eyes; whether this was an instinct to protect them from stone shards, or was simply out of fear, or perhaps shame, I cannot say, but I struck the chisel blind. From what I could make out in the torch light, the rock was unmarked. So I struck it again, this time with my eyes open and with greater force. I struck it again and again and again. The stone would not yield. A dull echo of the hammer's impact ran up my arm and twisted itself into the scarred flesh pinched around my shoulder.

I picked up the flashlight to assess these efforts and the bulb began to strobe. Then to my dismay it went out. The darkness it left was not one to which your eyes become accustomed. It was not an absence of light but a thing of form, massing around me and gently but firmly pushing me into the ground. I tried to straighten my legs, but they possessed that reluctance to move that has been the signature of my nightmares since returning from war.

As I struggled against this unknowable force, the flashlight began to flicker. Instead of offering me comfort from this dark paralysis, it plunged my brain into an impossible horror. For there, in those flashes of illumination, moved forms of such abhorrent size I cried out. I struggle even now to describe what I saw. I know with certainty they were taller than the treetops, pulsing and twisting with great speed, independent of the branches' response to the wind. Yet it was as if I were perceiving them without my eyes, as if some other more real sense was registering their presence in my brain. I knew they were ancient, older than the moorland itself, and lived in ways we have forgotten how to see. I knew also this was only the tangle of their shadow, that their true nature was buried somewhere within the hollow kingdom of the grey.

Like a child I shut my eyes. The shape of them came through the darkness behind my fastened lids. I cannot say how long I crouched there, frozen. Time had lost its grip on that place. I know only that my mind reached the very limit of resistance before it irrevocably splintered.

A warmth against my skin pulled me back from the abyss. I opened my eyes. The pattern on the rock before me glowed, a comet burning through the blackness of space. This fire spread until everything was aflame. It was beautiful. I was immediately overcome by an implacable compulsion to worship. The rock grew brighter and hotter, and I could feel my particles yearning to join, to be absorbed back into that violent angel of light. Opposite sensations gave way to one another with sudden rapid shifts; my consciousness was expanding, reaching infinitely out into the cosmos, and I was being scumfished, the last breath of air squeezed from my choking lungs.

Without warning the rock burst apart with a terrible crack. The force knocked me backwards onto the cold ground. With that, the light and the beings surrounding me were gone and I was alone once more in the darkness. The abstruse meaning of that thin, ancient place suddenly overwhelmed me, and I began to tremble dreadfully, overtaken again by a vast terror.

The torch stopped flickering and its beam returned bright and sharp, revealing the impact of the blast. The stone was all but destroyed, and the adjacent one badly damaged by shrapnel. Clarity returned at once. I pulled myself up from the ground and set about collecting as many rock fragments as the sample jars could afford.

A thin shard of stone had embedded itself in the back of my hand, dripping blood steadily onto the grass in the centre of the circle. I did not stop to stem the bleeding. After stuffing the jars into my knapsack, I scrambled back up the hill and down again into Birchover. Dawn was fast approaching, and the first rays of sunlight crept over the Derwent Valley. I had to get back to the Red Stag unknown and safely up into my room before the landlady rose."

PART TWO
THE JOURNEY

"Friend or foe is too reductive a question. Fungus and flower are so inextricably linked, they can scarcely be considered apart."
A Field Guide to the Woodland Floor, Andrew Forde, Chapelkill Press

Corpse flower

Even before the phone rang, I knew. More than a month
had passed since my last visit, despite their warnings time
was running out. Mum quickly forgave me, but Tom was
not so kind. He told me of Dad's lucidity at the end, how he
had cried out for me. He described his eyes, filled with hurt
and regret, when he saw I was not there to say goodbye.

The funeral was hard. I wrote a eulogy, but when the time
came, I could not get up and read it. Tom managed to, and
he managed to read mine. I bent forward, my head hung,
my back shuddering, as the hollow words I had scraped
out were scattered over me. The wake was no better, a
procession of dark strangers with sympathetic smiles and
tilted heads, waiting for the moment to express their
condolences – *He'll always be there if you keep him alive
in your memories.*

Tom continued to make it worse. He told me Dad visited
him every night in his dreams. He described how
reassuring it felt, how the connection between them had
not frayed. Dad had yet to visit me. Even with one of us
gone, the space between us was there.

I went back to Mum's after the wake and stayed there,
abandoning work, my studies, and my housemates. It was
comforting to be back in my childhood home. I quickly
came to appreciate the simple rhythm of life with Mum –
shopping in the morning, afternoon walks, soaps in the

evening. I could relieve my guilt by caring for her and helping her out around the house. Looking back, she was no doubt engineering her fragility for my sake, knowing it would help me recover. The vastness of my parent's love for me could be overwhelming. Grief would periodically creep up on me out of nowhere and my feet continued to itch unbearably, but on the whole, I grew more content than I had any right to be. I remember this time with clarity and fondness, despite other moments beginning to cloud.

Mum saved some of the lilies and orchids that smothered the house after the funeral, flattening them inside a large wooden flower press in the kitchen. The rest had wilted and died before I could bring myself to go into Dad's study. He had converted the attic himself when Tom and I were boys. Dad had never forbidden us from going up there, but we both knew that space was his. Though he tried to conceal it by leaning his head through the skylight, cigarette smoke would occasionally seep down into my bedroom. The smell was soothing, not intrusive, a reminder that Dad was up there.

It was a bright summer morning when I first opened the hatch. Mum had gone shopping, and the house was quiet. A faint hint of tobacco hit me as I stepped off the ladders. I sat on the attic floor and wept. My grief was selfish; I missed the way he made me feel – his big smile, his daft jokes, his random stories. I missed being a boy, I missed being cared for. My grief wasn't the nostalgic melancholy I had read about, it was brittle and invasive and hollowing.

The attic was huge, occupying the whole footprint of the house. The ceiling sloped on two sides in line with the angles of the roof. Along one side were six boxes of records pushed up against a partition wall. I picked myself up from the floor and flicked through a stack. There was Can, the Beatles, John Martyn, and Nick Drake, mixed with some jazz and classical albums, and a slew of prog odysseys with fantastic cover art. I chose a Pink Floyd LP and teed it up on the old record player in the corner. The instant those first notes rearranged the warm air, I slipped under a blanket on the back seat of Dad's car, lying side by side with Tom as we returned home from our grandma's house. Every mark on that record was captured on the chrome cassette Dad made for the journey, and every moment of that drive was held in those crackles and pops. It was always dark and often raining as we made our way over the White Peak. I would drift in and out of sleep, watching the headlights of oncoming traffic flicker across the inside of the car roof in sync with the clock chimes, drum strikes and heavy bass that vibrated through my bones. It was wonderful and frightening, like much of childhood.

Mum had yet to go through Dad's things. She had not been in the attic for some months, and everything was covered in a thin layer of dust. Over the next few weeks I spent hours up there, listening to records, reading books, and poking through memories of my father's life. Dad's presence was both reassuring and painful. There were maps of ley lines and ancient sites, journals about stone circles, and histories of folklore and witchcraft. You would struggle to accept he had been a physicist were you to assemble him from the tangle of his possessions.

The old straight track

Late one afternoon, as I was rifling through Dad's records, I noticed a series of low cupboards built into the partition wall behind the crates. I made some room and opened one of the little doors before dragging out a lidded box branded with RAF insignia. Dad had worked at Fylingdales in North Yorkshire when I was younger. My heart quickened when I spotted the "SENSITIVE" stamp on a heavy, spiral-bound manual. Its cover image was an aerial photograph of Fylingdales' giant golf balls, the three geodesic radomes that had squatted on the dark moorland like a lunar module from an out-of-date future. Dad would only talk obliquely about the base, how the peat on the moors would swallow the roads, or how the domes could listen to things that did not exist. He never spoke directly about his work there, earnestly citing the Official Secrets Act. For many years this was a source of persistent fascination for me, that he had been part of a project so classified he could not even share it with his children. The manual was not as revealing as I hoped. It was largely photographic, detailing the equipment used to predict missile impact, a fetishist catalogue of data cabinets, wiring, and control panels.

The box contained more manuals of incomprehensible circuitry diagrams and data processing sequences, the impossibly complex networks required to alert us of our four remaining minutes of life. At the bottom was a magazine called *Monolith*, "The Periodical of RAF Fylingdales". The image on the front cover was a dramatic shot of the SSPAR, the enormous pyramidal radar that has since replaced the three domes. It was an offbeat magazine, with profiles of weapons manufacturers, recipes, caption competitions, and a report from the wives' club. The inside of the back cover caught my breath. Dad's photograph made me laugh and cry at the same time. It was an American-style corporate shot, head turned slightly over his shoulder, big smile, white teeth. Though he would have found it excruciating, it was very flattering and made Dad look like a 1950s film star. The article described Dad's work dismantling the thousands of hexagons that formed the radomes, and the installation of the site's new radar system. That he had refused to tell me any of this but had shared it in a magazine carrying advertisements for balloon shops and quiltmakers made me a little resentful, until I reached the last question in the interview.

"Of what achievement are you most proud?
Creating my boys, the two most wonderful points in the universe."

Guilt and grief wrapped my arms about my head, and I sobbed into the fold of my elbow.

Another of the low cupboards contained a box of Dad's hiking attire, his compass resting on top. I sunk my face into a woollen hat. His aroma was so woven into my memories he came hurtling back to life, a cloud of aftershave, tobacco, and love.

Folded into a pile of knitted jumpers was a photograph album I had never seen. There were several pictures of Dad my age. I had come to resent being told how alike we were, but the resemblance was uncanny. Those images tricked my memory, reminding me of things that never took place. The last photograph captured Dad on his own, sitting cross-legged between the stone pillars of a dolmen. The print was overexposed and the sky above him burned. On the back, scrawled in fading biro, were the words *"THE COVEN STONE"*.

The scores of photographs pinned to the walls around Dad's desk were more familiar, an entire visual history of our family holidays, all there, all at once. Memories rushed to the surface, but they were just fragments, only those details caught on film. Maybe I was remembering the photographs themselves, not the days they captured.

One picture stood out and I unpinned it from the wall. St. Lythan's burial tomb was a short drive out from Cardiff, and Dad spent the entire journey telling us the folklore of the place. By the time we arrived I was terrified. Like Spinster's Rock, St Lythan's is a dolmen, or cromlech as they call them in Wales. It sits in a field known as the Accursed, on account of some baneful murrain that is said to spoil the fruit on the boughs, wither the crops in the earth, and infect the cattle that graze there. On the eve of the summer solstice, legend spins the capstone three times before the giant rocks drag themselves into the nearby river to bathe. Dad told us its Welsh name was *Gwal y Filiast*, "kennel of the greyhound bitch", a reference perhaps to local tale *Culhwch ac Olwen* in which King Arthur leads his hound on a wild hunt across the Welsh hills to slay a monstrous boar. The word bitch made Tom giggle uncontrollably, but the story only made me more afraid.

I was trembling when we got out the car and desperate not to show it to Tom. Mum and Dad laid their rug out in the shade of a giant oak. They watched us, holding hands and laughing to themselves. Six thousand years of wind and rain has weathered the cromlech, leaving the rocks lumpy and pockmarked, as if cursed by the dead beneath. I shrank away from that blighted stone, but I followed Tom inside. It was a tall structure, and we could stand up straight beneath the capstone. The low angle of the sun made it darker than I had anticipated. When my eyes adjusted, a mournful face leapt out from one of the uprights, its mouth hanging lifelessly open. I jumped back in shock. Tom let out a snort of derision and shook his head. The mouth was a hole cut through the rock. Tom dared me to put my hand in. The hole was some six feet up from the ground so I could not see through. Protected from the Welsh weather, the inner surface of the cromlech was smooth. With Tom egging me on, I leaned against the cold pillar and slowly raised my arm, skin tingling where it contacted stone. At last I reached the porthole and slid my hand into the space. I wiggled my fingers out through the other side and smiled at Tom triumphantly, before letting out a blood-curdling scream. Something had grabbed my wrist and was pulling me into the rock. Tom collapsed into exaggerated hysterics. Then the thing let me go.

Dad apologised repeatedly for scaring me, but there remained the trace of a smile on his face. I locked myself in the car and refused to get out. As a peace offering, Dad told me how I could get my revenge. If I returned on Halloween, the stones would grant any request whispered to them at the stroke of midnight. I never went back, but I did make a wish on the journey home, a terrible wish.

I wiped tears from my eyes and placed the photograph face down on one of the shelves above Dad's desk. The shelves were littered with found objects – driftwood, hag stones, fossils, arrow heads, dried mushrooms, tektite, antlers, feathers, and animal skulls. I reached up for a seashell and held it to my ear, remembering the warm Pembrokeshire waves that washed it ashore.

The rest of the attic was decorated with prints by Samuel Palmer, sketches of megaliths, and telescopic images of comets and supernovas. At the gable end was a gigantic chart of the British Isles. Dad would mark places he had visited with small black stars. Constellations were hidden in their arrangement on the map, but they refused to reveal themselves. Only one stood out. Ten or so of the stars joined together in a perfectly straight red line, creating a journey through Dad's memories that cleaved England in two, from South Devon all the way up to North Yorkshire. I recognised three of the sites at once – Spinster's Rock, St. Lythan's, and Doll Tor. There were numerous other stars along the track I was unfamiliar with before the pathway plunged into the sea somewhere along the coast near Whitby.

Crowfoot

It was Mum who persuaded me to go back to the Northcliffe. With only a week until Christmas, I would have time to recover after a couple of days' work. Not having formally agreed a leave of absence, I wasn't sure the library would take me back, but when I rang the Reading Room to enquire about my chances, William seemed to be expecting me. He was kind on the phone. He asked me how I was doing but did not press me when I offered little in the way of response. Things were swiftly arranged. I was to return on Monday. Not only that, William had a surprise for me.

I had been strangely anxious on the train from Marple. The moment I stepped into the Reading Room I was almost overcome with joy. It was like another homecoming. There was a handful of new faces amongst the readers and some decorative nods to Christmas, but otherwise the library was unchanged. I wandered from room to room and let the smell of old books and the sound of turned pages nudge me gently out the real world.

William was in the same spot I had left him on my final day six months ago, unpacking boxes of books and laying them out on a table. I observed him through the narrow window behind the main desk in the Reading Room. When at last he looked up and noticed me, he beckoned me over with a long, curled finger. I felt a rush of excitement as I lifted the hatch and let myself in behind the desk. He opened the door marked *LIBRARIAN* and shook my hand warmly.

William gave me some administrative tasks to get started – book shelving, the processing of inter-library loans, and searches for missing titles. When I returned to the library after my lunch break, he was sitting in the alcove beneath the statue of Hermes Trismegistus. He waved me over and explained my new assignment. The Northcliffe grew by acquiring other collections. William had received an offer from a public library near Whitby that had supplied the Northcliffe with titles in the past. They were still in possession of a significant number of interesting books and had neither the space nor the money to adequately house them. They were happy to give them to the Northcliffe for a small sum, to help pay for their upcoming festival. My job was to view the collection, catalogue it, and decide what titles would be of interest. There was a huge volume of books to go through and William estimated it would take three days, during which time I would be put up at a local inn. I would be returning home on Christmas Eve.

I stared blankly at the books behind William's head, large leather-bound histories of Bretagne and Carnac. Not so long ago, this mission would have been the best news William could have given me. I read a lot of books, but I owned far more that I never would. Many sat proudly on my shelves, many more were kept in boxes, moved from one house to the next, sometimes never opened. It was the hunt that thrilled me, digging through crates, scanning dusty shelves, studying number sequences on title pages for proof of a first edition. Though part of me was loathe to admit it, I was a collector; to get paid to do this on behalf of the Northcliffe should be a dream come true. And yet I was apprehensive. I was reluctant to leave the newfound security of my childhood home, and so close to Christmas. The task felt like an adventure, the scale of which I preferred to read about, not undertake myself.

"Do you think I am up to this? I have been off work six months."

"Of course you are. And I have put things in train. Vouched for you to the Board."

"Would you not be more suited to the task?"

"I'm afraid that's not possible. I am needed here."

"But surely you have the qualifications and experience required."

"As I said, I am needed here."

William's tone became curt, and a curious expression flashed across his face. It was no doubt impatience, but it looked like something else.

"Ok, well if you think I am able, then yes, of course."

"Splendid, splendid. You will find the town most rewarding."

"Have you visited there yourself?"

William did not answer. Instead, he lifted a large folder off his lap and slid it over the desk.

"So where am I going?"

"Chapelkill."

Separation

You don't forget a name like Chapelkill, though I could not immediately recall how I knew it. Searching for it in the library's map collection revealed nothing. I scanned the entire index and there were only two references to the town. The first was in an old compendium of British folk customs and described the endurance amongst locals of comet worship and ritualism. The second was a short article in a psychiatric journal outlining the therapy practiced at the town's medical foundation. As interesting as these accounts were, they were not the reason I was familiar with the town. I remembered when I got home. Dr Wistman refers to Chapelkill in his journal. It was where he purchased a breastpin for a woman who never received it, when his name and his life had been someone else's. An idea can grow in the mind at the expense of all others, and it was with unconscious relief I had abandoned my pursuit of the Doctor. Now it seemed fate had endeavoured to resume the hunt. I cannot say whether I was excited by this intervention or uneasy.

I was booked on the only direct train from Stockport. All others required a series of complicated and time-consuming changes in Sheffield, Doncaster, and Whitby. This one took me across the North York Moors, perhaps, by strange fortune, within sight of RAF Fylingdales. It departed just after eleven and Mum kindly agreed to drop me off at the station, giving me time to buy a couple of books for my trip.

Whilst the map of our family days out had been drawn through a network of standing stones and burial chambers, my own adventures have been charted from the location of secondhand book shops. I have visited scores of them across the country, but the best is a stone's throw from my childhood home. With a breakfast of poached eggs inside me, I set off through the spires of wych elm that climb up behind the house. The path cracked beneath my feet. It was completely covered, criss-crossed with sticks and branches, the scar tissue memory of a recent storm. A ghost of winter gnats rose from the undergrowth. It pulsed and flickered and swelled in the sharp morning sunlight. I followed this cloud of golden faeries through the trees before emerging onto the road that climbs steeply down into the village.

Talisman Books occupies a narrow two-floor building on Town Street, held together by dust and magic. *It's not for everyone,* reads the sign above the door. The lady who owns the shop knows my taste in books better than I do and always has something interesting stashed away for me. She wasn't there when I visited that morning. In her place at the desk by the window sat a tall, pale man with long unwashed hair, reading the newspaper and listening to some challenging electronic music a little too loudly. He seemed to know who I was and offered me a stack of books from the shelf above his head. I left with a field guide to the woodland floor and one of Merlyn Cullis's studies of stone circles.

We got to Stockport Station in good time. I had to persuade Mum not to wait with me on the platform. She had a tear in her eye when we hugged. Perhaps it was like losing Dad again. Watching me from the car park as I trudged towards the ticket office, she waved at me as if to a soldier on his way to the Front. Before turning the corner and out of sight I stopped to wave back, but she no longer appeared able to see me.

The sky looked like it wanted to snow when I shuffled onto the platform. There was a handful of people waiting with me, shivering. They all boarded the 10.56 to Piccadilly. Without looking up, the newsagent at the stand by the lifts held out his hand when I unfolded a copy of the Guardian. After paying him in coins I tucked the paper under my arm like a city gent from another time and stood on the platform edge.

I was looking up the line as a train rattled towards the station, an old diesel engine with maroon livery. I had not seen one like this since childhood. The heavy door required a firm yank down on the handle before I could open it and step into the carriage's narrow corridor. Along the corridor was a series of empty stalls, each with six burgundy seats, three front-facing, three rear-facing. I found the correct stall and slid open the door. My seat was by the window, looking back. I heaved my bag into the luggage rack above and flopped down. There were two pictures attached to the wall in front of me. They were mezzotints - a giant stag standing proudly amongst moorland heather, and a wild boar grazing on mushrooms beside a wooded stream. The seat was worn and sun-bleached, but softly sprung velvet cushioning and a perfectly placed headrest curling about my face made it effortlessly comfortable. I opened the curtains drawn across the window and gathered them in their tiebacks. There was a shrill whistle and the train pulled wearily from the station. A long satisfying yawn crept out and I smiled as I made myself snug.

For the next hour and a half, I drifted in that blissful hypnagogic state between waking and sleep. I can recall little of my dreams, only feelings, of stone and root and stars. Through the window, valleys and streams and woodland rolled past, and the carriage's gentle rocking mixed them seamlessly into my own creations. It went on forever. I was safe on the train, safe in my head, and the happiest I had felt for months. By the time I woke up I was miles from home. That you can physically travel in your dreams is something wonderful.

Conjunction

Standing up to stretch, I retrieved my bag from the luggage rack above and pulled its contents out onto the seat beside me. On top was Dad's compass. He had doggedly tried to teach me map reading with that instrument so I would never find myself lost. It was inextricably linked to him in my memories, no doubt the reason I had chosen to bring it.

Sliding the compass into my jacket pocket, I turned my attention to the thick folder William had prepared. I removed its contents and placed them on the small table sticking out from beneath the window. The folder carried several documents, including a blank log book, a page of contacts in Chapelkill, and detailed instructions regarding the volumes I was to search for at Rooksnest. Underneath this pile of papers was an old leather-bound journal tied around with string. After carefully unpicking the knot, I opened the cover. A powdery jet spurted up from the page and I was overwhelmed by the smell of mould, old paper, and something like sulphur. Momentarily light-headed, I felt the carriage slip away from me. As quickly as it arrived the sensation faded and I was back on the train, dust tickling my nostrils, my vision slightly blurred. Handwritten text on the title page swam slowly into focus – *The Comb, by Doctor Alfred Wistman*.

I snapped the journal shut and tossed it onto the seat beside me. I had partly blamed my interest in Dr Wistman for Dad's death. Whilst I knew this to be irrational, I could not deny I had allowed it to erode any responsibilities I had as a son. Why had William given me it? I cursed him but could not forget the pressure I had applied to give me those microfiche sheets in the first place.

For the next twenty minutes I ignored the journal and stared out the window or leafed through the books I had purchased that morning. Merlyn Cullis's study of stone circles is part of the Village Archaeology range. It is a fascinating study, but I struggled to keep my focus. I turned instead to the Guardian. Annoyingly it was a couple of days out of date. I flicked through the paper to the science section. A small article described astronomers' surprise and delight at the imminent return of a supernova first seen in the sixteenth century. Still my mind wandered.

Regardless of what I tried to persuade myself, I was desperate to learn the identity of Dr Wistman before he had gone to war, before he had chosen to transform himself. It was between the pages of the journal on the seat beside me I had the best chance of finding out. Having spent so much time immersed in Alfred's work, I could almost hear him, his contempt for my deliberate ignorance, his disappointment with me for not seeing it through. Eventually Dr Wistman's was the loudest voice in my head, and I snatched the journal from the seat beside me.

Until now I had only seen reproductions of Alfred's studies on sheets of film. His words had been shrunk to such a microscopic size they required a machine to be plugged in, switched on, and warmed up before they held any meaning. This had given his work an unreal, fictional quality, allowing fascination to grow into obsession from a point of relative safety. Now that I held one of Dr Wistman's journals in my hand, his words were all too real. He was too real. Somewhere, far away, I could almost feel him come to life. It filled me with a strange thrill, not altogether pleasant.

Instead of launching straight in I flicked through the journal cautiously. Its pages were deckled, with rough uncut edges. Towards the back were things missing from the microfiche archive, beautiful things. Beneath thin waxen leaves was a collection of pressed wildflowers, alphabetically arranged – bryony, foxglove, hellebore, hemlock, henbane, lily, mandrake, monk's hood, nightshade, rosemary, stonecrop, thistle, and yarrow, their petals, leaves, and stems flattened into two dimensions. So bright were they, so clear, so vivid, they felt more alive than if they had been in the ground. They were distilled to their very essence until they burned from the page. It was breathtaking, almost overwhelming.

Without warning the carriage plunges into darkness. There is a terrible scream, like the roar of a moorland storm. Only it is infinitely louder and harsher, and is coming from within me, not without. With no other senses to call on I am deafened. I cry out, but my shriek is lost in black thunder. A flash of brilliant white light makes me blink. Then it goes quiet. We are through the mountain.

Earthstar

Dr Wistman's journal picks up shortly after his trip to Stanton. Following a series of confrontations with fellow academics and "contemptuous accusations of erratic behaviour", Alfred's studies became the focus of speculation at the Pennine Institute and across the universities at which he taught. He was reluctant to share his work with his benefactors and his trips to Woodhead Reservoir became increasingly less frequent. I speculated as to why the Institute afforded him so much leeway. His reputation perhaps? Sympathy maybe? They offered to procure him psychiatric intervention for the treatment of shellshock, but Alfred declined, referencing the practice in his journal with both fear and contempt. He found solace in fishing and considered his work and its documentation a form of therapy.

"I am thankful for this journal. To write a thing down is to capture it. Once you have trapped it on the page you can analyse a thing, make sense of it."

The Institute helped Dr Wistman by providing him the space he requested to work out of hours. Whilst he spent much of his day at Chetham's, at night Alfred worked from a vacant laboratory in the basement of Manchester Museum. The nature of his work during this time is not easy to decipher from his entries, but an unwavering admiration for John Dee is clear.

"Dee's use of the black mirror is well documented. Gazing on the surface of this scrying glass, the Doctor believed he could see into the future and converse with angels. Many dismiss him for such unscientific pursuits. But Dee was more than a mere occultist. He was the first to see mathematics as the universal language, the literal building blocks of our universe. In 1573 he published *Parallacticae commentationis praxosque*, which demonstrates the trigonometric methods he used to calculate the distance of a star that had appeared suddenly in the night sky. Tycho's Supernova was first observed in 1572 by a handful of contemporary astronomers including Tycho Brae, after whom the supernova was named."

I put the journal down and flicked back through the science section of the Guardian. There it is again, Tycho's Supernova. Its remains will be visible to the naked eye tomorrow night, December 21st. Those on higher ground along the eastern edge of the country will have the best chance of seeing it. This blurring of our stories made me a little uncomfortable.

"Known as *The Phenomenon*, the star appeared in the constellation of Cassiopeia. It was the brightest object in that region of the sky, often still visible in daylight. If this was a new celestial object, it transformed reality. The great outer orb of the universe, fixed since the beginning of Creation, had shifted. Ptolemy and Aristotle declared the universe unchanging, and this was the accepted truth amongst scholars and the Church. The appearance of a new star cast doubt over everything that was known about the cosmos.

Dee's theory for the appearance of this new astronomical body was radical to the point of heresy. The star's brilliance grew and shrunk suggesting to Dee it was moving. This implied the star was not attached, that there was a space beyond the celestial sphere into which it could travel, a space that was unquestioned and untouchable – heaven itself.

To aspire to meet Dee's vision, to equal the bravery of his conviction, must surely be the aim of every scientist and thinker. Without her, it is this goal, and this goal alone, that carries me aloft through the incessant loneliness and mediocrity of this world. I must be unwavering in my conviction; I must steel myself to confront that which is asked of me; I must burn that ambition into my heart as Lucifer did his hoof on my study table. For if I fail, will it not all have been for naught?"

Kinder Downfall

Engrossed in the journal, I was startled when he entered the stall. He nodded almost imperceptibly, and I smiled back, a little embarrassed. Without any luggage to store he sat straight down in the seat diametrically opposite mine. As he stared ahead, I took the opportunity to study him through the corner of my eye. He was a short, thick-set man, his rolled-up sleeves revealing impossibly broad forearms. He wore old-fashioned black trousers tucked into dirty shin-high boots and held up by braces, pulled tight over a crisp white shirt. His face was clean-shaven, and his hair cropped short to the scalp. A largely invisible tattoo crept out from his collar and up the side of his neck to the jaw line. Though hard to make out, it looked like a snake curling around a sphere. Thankfully he did not seem interested in making conversation, so I returned to Dr Wistman's journal.

Alfred reproduced John Dee's esoteric diagrams with great care – *The Seal of God*, *The Vision of the Four Castles*, *The Table of Practice.* Dee had published numerous accounts of his experiments and meticulously collected the works of others with the same sacred knowledge. His library at Mortlake was perhaps the greatest collection of its kind. When Dee returned home from his travels around Europe at the end of the sixteenth century, however, he found it ransacked, every title stolen or destroyed. Throughout his journal, Wistman reveals a devotion to tracking down the remnants of this collection, an obsession I recognised at once. He frequently references the one book that continued to elude him, *Mercurius Coelestis*, Dee's accounts of his own alchemical practice.

"It is all in that book, all of it; I know this to be true. I have read it in my dreams, in the light of the fire, cold skin cover in my hands. I turn the pages, one by one, and remember what I already know. She is at the end, hidden in the last plate. But I never reach it before morning. Still, I learn a little more each night. We grow closer."

As well as a preoccupation with Dee, Wistman's journal demonstrates a growing fascination with mushrooms and Apoidea. Following this new direction in Alfred's work, the

Museum reported incidents of mould outbreaks, bee infestations, and acrid smells from his saprotrophic experiments with the fungal decomposition of dead matter. This brought Dr Wistman a degree of scrutiny he was unable to endure, so he began to seek out new facilities that would provide both the privacy and space his increasingly unconventional research demanded. In 1937 he placed an application with the Pennine Institute to purchase a parcel of land twenty miles south of Manchester at Blackden Carr, in the heart of the East Cheshire countryside.

The journal entry admits his submission lacked basic detail and would likely fail to meet the necessary criteria. As he expected, it was not enough to satisfy the Board's Treasurer that such a purchase was in the best interests of the Institute, and Dr Wistman's application was rejected. Still, by 1938, on the eve of the second world war, the land was his.

Events surrounding this change of policy are unclear, but attached to the opposite page of Alfred's journal was a folded, yellowing article, clipped from the *Glossop Mail* – "*Pennine Institute mourns; Treasurer found dead*". The article recounted the discovery of the Treasurer's body at the top of Kinder Scout on Christmas Eve 1937. Every bone in his body had been shattered. I know Kinder Scout well. For several years Dad would take us up there on the weekends he was not away with work. He could effortlessly navigate us through that boggy peatland in the most treacherous conditions. Only one time, just after his diagnosis, was I concerned. Visibility was reduced to the end of my fingers, and we huddled around a map while Dad tried to take readings with his compass. The needle twitched randomly, and he grew increasingly impatient as the thick cold fog pressed itself against us. Then his hand started shaking. The compass tapped against the map like someone knocking on a door hidden in the mist. When he looked up at me his eyes were filled with fear and confusion.

Kinder Downfall drops some thirty metres onto the hard gritstone plateau below. Lose your footing on that damp edge of the Pennines and there is a long way to fall. According to his obituary the Treasurer was not so lucky. His broken body was found not at the bottom of the waterfall, but at the top.

Vigilamus

At some point I came to sense the scrutiny of the other passenger. I ignored his attention for as long as I was able, waiting for him to look away. His observation continued and I started to lose focus. Eventually I made a point of re-positioning myself, as if trying to get comfortable in my seat. This gave me the opportunity to look up at him with the appearance of chance. He was staring right at me. Nodding stiffly, I returned to the journal.

"How's the enemy?"

"What?"

"The time, what is it?"

I looked down at my watch. The hands were stilled.

"I'm sorry, my watch appears to have stopped."

The man nodded before pulling a deck of cards from his trouser pocket and fanning it into a circle.

"Do you want to see a trick?"

"Thank you but no. I must finish my reading."

"You look the type. If you don't mind my saying."

Hoping this would be an end to it, I stared down at the journal, but I could feel his eyes still on me. I looked up again and smiled awkwardly.

"Reckon an onion on your pillow would draw a blank." He laughed to himself and continued on before I could express my confusion. "Home for the holidays son?"

"Actually I'm here on business."

"Not been into Chapelkill before I'll stake."

"No, it's my first visit."

"It always is."

"No-one goes back again. Is that it?"

"Something like that. What can you want in the village?"

For a moment I had to think.

"I'm there to look at a collection of books."

"I'm sure you are."

"Do you know Chapelkill?"

"Everyone knows it round here."

"Perhaps you could tell me something of the place?"

I took his impassive silence as consent to continue.

"What do you know of a Doctor Wistman?" He continued to stare at me, unspeaking. "I understand he used to—"

"He collects things. Sets them to work."

"What things?"

"If it's him you're after you'll do well to go straight through to Whitby. Visit the museum, take in the sea."

"I'm not sure I'll have time."

"There'll be plenty of that."

"Well I've a lot to do. I'm purchasing quite a valuable library."

"Are you now?"

"You'll have to excuse me; I need to get back to my reading."

The train started to slow, and the man stood up to leave.

"When they start the Hunt, which are you?"

I looked at him blankly and he nodded to the prints of the stag and the boar above the seats in front of me.

"I don't understand."

"No, you don't. You should keep on this train 'til Whitby."

"I'll bear that in mind."

"Aye, you do that."

After this stop the train began to climb slowly up onto the moors. My breath left a cloud on the window that I wiped away with my sleeve to observe patches of pale grasses flanking the tracks become replaced by bracken and then by gorse and then finally by dark heather when we reached Snod Hill. Snow bones hugging dry stone walls and lining shakeholes crept out from their shelters and joined to form a great blanket of sparkling ice. From this cold blank page, a dark pyramid reared up into the sky. It was difficult to judge its size as it was some distance from the train, but it seemed to be everywhere, all at once. With no other vertical lines within that white featureless landscape, it was an impossible, terrible thing, too big and too out of place to be real. Yet it was beautiful by the very nature of its incongruousness. A flush of pride warmed me as I considered Dad, working on the construction of that modern megalith, bringing its secret magic to life. I watched it for a long time until it dipped from sight. For what little I had left of my journey, I returned to Alfred's journal.

Space face

The nature of Dr Wistman's research at Blackden Carr is not clear from his journal. There is little in it I could understand from a biological or geological perspective. Long passages are written using a cipher. Elsewhere Alfred dips into Latin, cuneiform script, and symbols I did not recognise.

The fragments I could understand reveal plans for a system of trenches dug into the earth and connected into a giant hexagon two hundred feet in diameter. Alfred refers to this excavation as "the Comb". His detailed illustrations identify the position of the sun on the morning of the winter solstice, as well as Pythagorean methods for the even distribution of fungal spawn and the rock shards he had taken from Doll Tor. His technique was difficult to understand, but it used the hole of a hag stone for perspective, six hundred yards of twine, and a wooden staff, cut exactly to his own height. The purpose of the Comb is equally vague, but what Alfred's narrative lacks in clarity it makes up for with enthusiasm.

Within six months of Alfred's relocation, the Pennine Institute began to receive complaints from the police about light and noise pollution at night. Britain was once again in the grip of a world war and the Institute could dismiss much of this unusual activity as part of the Luftwaffe strikes against Liverpool and Manchester. A disproportionate number of reports came from Northwich, Knutsford, Alderley Edge, Macclesfield, Congleton and Sandbach, the six towns and villages that when connected on a map, locate Blackden Carr at their centre. Shortly after the end of the war, the RAF scrambled from their base at Church Fenton in response to sightings of unusual lights in the skies above Goostry. After that, Dr Wistman's story took another turn.

Alfred was informed of his fate by letter. Following a series of accidents, fires and the downturn of their respective businesses, the industrialists funding the Pennine Institute were keen to claw back some of their investment. The

Board voted unanimously to sell the land at Blackden Carr to the Astronomy Department of the Manchester Albert University. Out of respect, or perhaps something other, the Institute secured Alfred another five years to conclude his studies. He would have full access to the site and its facilities but would be a guest there.

Alfred describes the physicists' arrival with thinly disguised fear. He watched as they unpacked giant crates in his field and assembled alien metal structures with naval and air force equipment left over from the war. Dr Wistman had spent much of the last thirty years digging into the ancient past. Seeing the future built around him plunged his brain into an existential terror.

It was almost with sympathy I considered Alfred's plight; but there was someone else more deserving. The telescope the university would build at Blackden Carr evolved continuously over the years, and we had visited it many times. He would gaze with awe when it climbed over the horizon like a moon. You could plot Dad's life with that bowl of white noise, tracking satellites and probes and masers and quasars. It had even searched for terrestrial threats before his own work at Fylingdales returned it to the stars. Dad spoke of it with wonder in his voice, marvelling as it connected with other stations to form MERLIN, a networked hexagon of radioscopic leys reaching further and further into our past. Dad would have been as fascinated with Alfred's journal as I was. It wasn't fair.

PART THREE
THE RITUAL

"Networks flow, above and below, in every direction and back.
Perhaps so it is with time."

The Comb, Doctor Alfred Wistman

Hola weg

Chapelkill is a desolate station, cut into the side of a steep hill. I had barely stepped down onto the platform and closed the carriage door before the train hurried quickly away over the moors. The space it left was filled by a ferocious gust of wind and ice that rushed up from the valley and tore into my face. Everything on the platform was in motion, shaking, rattling, banging. Just as suddenly the wind dropped, and everything was still.

I looked around, eyes narrowed. The station was empty. There were a couple of concrete benches, an abandoned ticket office, and a gloomy waiting room, its doors chained shut. Every surface was gliddered with a thin layer of frost, obscuring detail and reducing the scene to an unfinished sketch. This lack of rendering spread beyond the station and up the snow-covered hillside. Trees and fields and stone walls sat on the landscape like a fog and bled upwards into the winter sky. Here was the very edge of things. Only the horizon provided any contrast. The radomes at Fylingdales were three giant orbs, glowing red in the dying sun. Lying in bed that night, I realized my mistake.

The impatient darkness of December was closing round, and I was keen to get into town. I followed the words *Way Out* into the huffling wind. It relented again as I crossed the tracks and negotiated a kissing gate on the other side. A single icicle hung from the top bar. I snapped it off, cracking the air with a sudden violence that was smothered at once by the woodland in front of me. In the other direction the mournful cry of a curfew carried over the moors on a flurry of snow. That lonely bird should have moved down to the shelter of the marsh or estuary by now. Maybe its family had died or had left it behind. I shivered and turned up the collars of my coat.

Attached to the gate was a metal fingerpost, crossed by two arrows. One was blank and looked out over the moorland; the other said *This Way* and pointed into a deep holloway, curving gently downwards through the trees. Tall banks of exposed earth and twisted roots climbed over my head. These steep cliffs were tangled with ivy, hart's tongue, and gossamer blankets of spider silk frosted with ice. Leaning inwards and interlacing like fingers, the trees on either side created a thick ceiling of branches and withered leaves that dripped melting icicles like rain. Mistletoe balls nested between them, an orrery of ragged black stars and pale moons. All around me birds cried, and the undergrowth crackled quietly with the trample of tiny feet.

With every step, the vaulting of elder trees, hornbeam, alder, and hawthorn thickened and lowered, and the harrowed path grew darker. Before long I had to walk with a stoop to avoid tangling my hair in the branches above. This frozen memory of a path was slippery and uneven, and my blistered feet pressed uncomfortably into the toes of my boots. I considered turning back but had passed no other exit from the woods.

I hit the sunken road with some force and knocked the air from my lungs. Struggling to breathe, I allowed panic to rush through my veins. A sharp pain in my leg quickly supplanted this anxiety with fury and I cursed loudly, rolling over onto my back. It was cold and black on the ground, and I fumbled in my pocket for the small torch attached to my keyring. My trousers had ripped open, exposing a bright red lump pushing up through the mud on my knee. Dragging myself into a sitting position, I looked around to see what had tripped me. The torchlight picked out a small arrow-shaped sign, no more than a foot above the path. *Chapelkill was c*arved into the wood in an unfamiliar font. The sign pointed down a short tunnel of earth and root and branch. I crawled into that dark silence on all fours and forced my way out through a hawthorn tree at the end.

Ouroboros

I found the library down a side street off the market square. According to the town hall clock, my meeting with the head librarian was in ten minutes, and I was a little self-conscious at the state of my clothing. I need not have worried. When I got there, I found the entrance locked shut. For a brief moment I saw Dad beyond the glass doors, staring back at me with surprise. My heart leapt and

I took a step towards him before I noticed the rip on the left knee of his trousers.

I placed my hand on the glass. It vibrated slightly and there was a low humming coming from inside. I peered through the door. Within a couple of metres, any light spilling in from the street was overwhelmed, revealing only a fan of unopened mail and a scattering of dry leaves across the floor. It appeared the library had been closed for some time.

Mounted asymmetrically to the wall beside the entrance was a glass-fronted community board. Unsure what to do next, I gazed absently through dust and cobwebs to the notices stapled onto faded green felt.

"Poison, medicine, monocle for the third eye. Join us at the village hall for an appreciation of fungus with the Reverend Burntknight."

Beneath this was a flyer for the library's weekly Palmistry Night. Run by local mystic and lollipop lady Sally Whitbarrel, it offered full readings for five pounds. Discounts were available for people with missing fingers.

"Light refreshments and heavy mime will be provided".

At the bottom of the board was a yellowing note sellotaped to the glass. The ink was smudged and difficult to read, but it appeared to be addressed to me.

"To the librarian from the Northcliffe. Apologies, time has caught up with us. Please make your way to the Drab Tooth across the square. We have made arrangements

*for your stay and for your carriage to Rooksnest Manor
where much of the collection resides. We are _____. Good
luck. Your friend, the Head Librarian.*"
I shook my head and sighed. It was becoming apparent
why William had chosen not to come here.

I limped across the cobbled market place, passing
between an old well and a large boulder resting in a metal
frame. The well was a simple stone cylinder, decorated
around its entire circumference. I had seen well-dressing
before in Buxton and Eyam, but never so late in the year.
A wooden lattice frame had been constructed around the
stones and daubed with clay. This clay was a canvas,
adorned with flowers, seeds, mosses and berries, creating
the night sky, dominated by a giant comet. It was vividly
rendered in red and yellow and white petals stretching
around the well and back again, a snake eating its own
tail. The comet's head was animal-like, with flaming antlers
and tusked jaws. I gazed at it for some time before the
crash of spilled wares and a stallholder's angry curse
broke the spell.

Across the top of the well, a wrought iron crow served as a
grate to stop people tumbling in. It was a long way down
and black as pitch, with no shimmer of water at the
bottom. After removing a penny from my pocket, I dropped
it into the darkness. Before I made a wish I waited for a
faint splash or the echoed chink of the coin striking cold
stone. There was only silence.

The boulder beside the well was large and had the shape of an inverted, slightly flattened pyramid. Actually, it was closer to a giant chanterelle mushroom, fossilised, with vertical ridges like gills along its sloping undersides. Covered in patches of different lichens, the rock was a glorious swirl of oranges and silvers and greens. Meeting the ground at its narrowest point, it sat in a hexagonal iron support, some twenty inches across and fifteen inches in height. Widening circles of cobbles radiated outwards, as if the town had been built around the rock. Beside it, a small hand-painted wooden sign leaned out from the ground.

The Bolide Stone

Ring your finger round the stone,
Stone shall linger skin and bone.

It seemed foolish to pass the opportunity, so I gently drew a circle on the lichen with the end of my finger. The stone tipped gently back and forth, the edges of its pointed base alternately striking different sides of the iron hexagon. Each side made a slightly different sound, creating a repeating six-note melody that echoed around the market square. Conscious of stallholders' sudden interest in me, I glanced furtively round for the inn.

There were three pubs overlooking the market place. Thankfully the Drab Tooth looked the most attractive and I hobbled towards it through the wintry twilight. It was a tall thin building with convex windows bulging out into the square. The door was low and narrow, and I ducked inside.

The landlord

"What will it be?"

"Do you have any cask ales? Or an east coast IPA perhaps?"

"We've got what you'll see in front of you."
I had never heard of the beers on offer and the landlord did not seem keen to describe their relative merits. I picked one with a picture of a toadstool attached to the pump.

"I'll try the Holy Fire."
The landlord looked down at my torn trousers before nodding and pouring a particularly dark beer into a plain ceramic tankard.

"You the librarian?"

"That's me, yes."
It seemed pointless correcting him that I was merely a library assistant. Besides, mine was the work of a librarian's, so I do not believe this was stretching the truth.

"You'll have to do."

"I'm sorry?"

"William not joining you?"

"No, he can't afford the time."

"Figures. I'm to drive you to Rooksnest in the morning."

"Excellent. What can you tell me of the house?"

"It's a thin place. Things get stuck there."

I smiled at his dramatically ominous response. He did not smile back.

"Is there anything else I should know?"

"It's older than it is now. Always been there."

I made a sound suggesting I understood. The landlord looked back at me impassively.

"Well, I'm cataloguing a large number of interesting books. I'm led to believe it's quite a significant collection."

"No doubt."

"You interested in antiquarian texts?"

"No sense reviving forgotten horrors."

I could not suppress a nervous laugh. He stared at me with the same blank expression.

"If that's all, I'll be getting your room prepared. I'll knock on for you shortly before five."

"Five? In the morning?"

"If it doesn't suit, we can call time on the undertaking. You'll find no-one else round-abouts to take you."

"Ok, that will be fine I guess."

"You eaten?"

"No, not yet."

"I'll send Elizabeth over with a menu."

I found a small table in front of the fireplace. A large black cat lay curled on the hearth and watched me through one eye as I collapsed wearily into a high-backed armchair. The lounge was dressed for Christmas. Garlands of silver bells and bright paper chains hung from a low ceiling, and the thick, uneven walls were draped with festoons of holly and mistletoe. In one corner a great tree grew through the stone flags. Huge baubles decorated its branches, their clear glass revealing bright tangles of thread inside. Perched on top was a delicately carved wooden boar.

Flames roaring in the grate quickly got to work on the pain throbbing through my bruised knee. The beer was particularly good, rich and malty, and slipped down too easily. Beyond the frosted windows darkness had fallen completely. The world was reduced to this one room. It was wonderful. As I waited for the waitress to bring over a menu, I pulled Dr Wistman's journal from my bag.

Putrefaction
Whilst much of his own research from this time is undocumented, Dr Wistman's journal frequently references the physicists at Blackden Carr and their search for the anomalous echoes their radar equipment was recording in the sky.

"They look up for their complex patterns of truth, but they will never see it all. It is just as much in the earth beneath their feet. These astronomers are the magi of our day. Magic became religion and religion became science. Spells became miracles became processes. But one did not replace the next. The former is always there, waiting, like an atavistic gene.

Still, their vision of the cosmos was inspiring. Yesterday is not lost but is here with us now. So long does a star's radiance take to reach our eye, its past remains in the future. Time is not a single, moving point, but an impossibly complex network joining different points in space. All of history exists there above us, all at once. Meticulously have I mapped the lines of our ancient stones. If such leys run through time also, could one not learn to follow these parallel latitudes forwards and back? Perhaps this is how I shall find her."

From this point onwards Dr Wistman's journal becomes increasingly difficult to read. So quickly did he commit his thoughts to paper, his handwriting often collapses, letters and words blurring into a single line, meaningless to all but their author. Where form does return to Alfred's text, I have quoted it in full. Where words are illegible, I have taken the liberty to second guess, or to insert my own. I have spent so long in the corners of Alfred's mind I feel uniquely placed to do this truthfully and accurately.

"How are we sir?"
For the second time that day, I was so engrossed in Dr Wistman's research, I visibly jumped at someone's unnoticed arrival. I looked up at her and she smiled back at me, amused by my reaction. She was very pretty, with cropped blonde hair and piercing blue eyes. I ignored her question, hoping to regain control.

"The landlord told me you would give me a menu."

"I will, yes."

She stood there unmoving, with an ambiguous smile on her face.

"Ok, what's on the menu?"

"There's meat pie sir."

"Yes?"

She went quiet again, suggesting that was the menu.

"I'll have the meat pie then please."

"Very good sir. It comes with potatoes and mushrooms."

"Thank you."

"Who is you?"

I was taken aback by her abrupt and unusually constructed question. Her accent was difficult to place. Maybe English wasn't her first language.

"My name is—"

"That's not what I meant sir."

"Oh."

"Are you going to be the librarian?"

"I *am* the librarian."

"An important role."

"Yes, I like to think so."

"Where are you from?"

"From?"

"Yes."

"Manchester. I'm from Manchester."

"What's it like?"

"It's…well, you know…busy I suppose."

"Why are you here?"

"I'm cataloguing a library of books up at Rooksnest. Do you know it?"

"Of course. All our stories are in there."

"Yes, I understand it's quite a collection."

It went quiet. She stood there staring at me, not speaking.

"So, are you into books?"

"I don't know what you mean sir." And she laughed happily.

I blushed. "I just wondered if you liked to read?"

"There's more to life than reading sir, begging your pardon."

"Very true. It's good to learn new things though."

"And old."

"Quite."

"They won't let you take them."

"Take what?"

"The books."

"We are buying them. We're not stealing them."

"And you are willing to pay?"

"Well, yes, I am. That's why I'm here."

"Gravy."

"Gravy?"

"Gravy. With your pie?"

"Er yes, gravy."

She walked away laughing, leaving me wondering what had just taken place.

The beer eventually worked its way through and a visit to the toilet became pressing. I found the gents at the end of the bar, on the other side of the cigarette machine. Attached to the wall between the hand towel and the urinal was an enormous glass cabinet, the kind used to display stuffed animals, or birds, or fish. This one was bare, lacking even the details expected to bring a scene to life – no branches, no reeds, no background painting of a wood or river bank. It was an empty case, its description on a small brass plaque scratched out. The whole thing was a little disconcerting and made me wonder what or who they intended to put in there. Unless of course they had just removed its contents and I was about to eat it for supper.

My fears proved unfounded, and the generic meat pie turned out to be excellent, if in need of a little more salt. The giant cat on the hearth sat up and studied me haughtily as I ate. I managed another pint with my meal and ordered a brandy to wash it down. Elizabeth brought my drink over on a tray, along with a small bowl of plum pudding and a key attached to an enormous rabbit's foot.

"Yours is room number two. On the second floor."

"Thank you. Can I ask what your cat's called?"

"That's Slippery Jack."

"He's quite a specimen."

"We were sad to hear about your father."

"How do you mean?"

"Him passing."

"Ok. Thank-you, yes."

"He'll always be there if you keep him alive in your memories."

"So they say."

"They sometimes return in the Hunt."

"What?"

I was too shocked to call her back, too shocked to be angry. This came later in my room. It seemed William had shared my personal information with the Head Librarian, who had clearly shared it with the landlord, who had seemingly shared it with all and sundry.

My frustration was confused by the sudden peel of a bell for last orders. It carried on after the landlord had stopped ringing. No longer did it come from the bar, but from outside, from a church somewhere on the edge of the market place. Upon hearing it, the customers in the lounge immediately put down their drinks and marched out into the night. I looked around. The room was empty save for the landlord who remained behind the bar drying pots.

"What's going on?"

"The Dancing of the Yule."

"Are you not joining them?"

"You've to be invited to join the Hunt. There's no role for me."

I smiled at this, an expression somewhere between sympathy and confusion. The landlord did not smile back.

"I think I'll take a look."

The church bells suddenly stopped.

"Mind how you go."

King's crown

The town square was transformed, thronged with a writhing mass of people. They were singing and dancing, many were beating drums or shaking tiny bells on sticks; others carried burning torches that flickered light over the dancers' rapt faces as they slipped in and out of darkness. All of them wore the same expression. It was mesmerising, somewhere between ecstasy and pain. The gentle clang of their bells echoed against the cobbled floor and the stone buildings surrounding the market place. Beneath this was a faint six-note melody. The music fed back on itself in repeating loops until the vibration of the air became a net around us. It could have been a discordant sound, but it was curiously soporific. I stood there for some time, transfixed by a pleasant awe. Then everything stopped.

The crowd fell silent and parted in two. At the front of each group was a line of torchbearers. A channel of light between them revealed the well and the Bolide Stone and two costumed figures standing motionless in the space between. One wore antlers and a long mask of leaves and sticks. The other had the head of a boar, with huge tusks and coarse black bristles about its face. Both were dressed in robes, long sheets of red, orange, yellow and white cloth cut into vertical strips. They were naked beneath, the boar a man, the stag a woman.

A slow drum beat broke the silence, growing faster with every strike. The boar and the stag swayed in time with this quickening beat and the crowd began to chant, a single persistent note that grew louder and higher until the two costumed figures leapt into the air and the market place roared. Incited by the crowd, the two figures continued to leap and spin. Every time they left the ground the strips of their coloured robes billowed out behind them like fiery tails, exposing their naked midriffs to the delight of the villagers. Music and dancing started up again and the congregation collapsed into a whole once more. Climbing to impossible heights, the boar and the stag floated through a cloud of tributes tossed into the black sky. I looked down at my feet. The cobbles were flowing with thousands of nuts and berries and tiny shells.

From the tail of my eye, I became aware of someone's gaze. I looked up to find Elizabeth watching me from the edge of the square. She wore a floor-length white dress, and a wig of long black hair fell from the scarlet bonnet fastened to her head. Mistletoe sprigs were attached to her arms in which she clutched an enormous bread loaf, baked into the shape of an animal of some kind. Smiling at me happily, she span round and skipped into the dance. All at once the revellers fell still and parted again, revealing an enormous log, bound with metal chains. Elizabeth approached the felled tree slowly and placed the loaf on top. She removed her bonnet and tied it around. From somewhere within the folds of her dress she pulled a long knife and raised it over her head. It sparkled in the quivering torch light before she plunged it into the bread.

Behind her the man dressed as a boar dropped to the ground dramatically and a huge cheer rang out. Four of the male villagers lifted him from the cobbles, raising him onto their shoulders. The girl in the stag costume stepped forward before untying Elizabeth's bonnet from the broken loaf and stuffing it into the snout of his mask. Another cheer rang out and the man-boar was placed belly down on the log, his limbs hanging limply over the sides. A third girl emerged from the crowd, tall and willowy, and strong like a tree. She cast a large net of red rope around the man-boar and fastened it around each of his legs. The four men picked up the trunk's metal chains before dragging it slowly across the square and into the night. Music and dancing started up again and the villagers followed this strange procession. I listened until the echo of their wassailing faded upwards into the dark winter sky.

Star thistle

My room on the second floor was basic but perfectly adequate. There was a desk and chair beside the window, a large wooden wardrobe, a double bed, and a bathroom. Dotted around were several vases of dried flowers. Hanging from the wall was a large photograph in a bright red frame. It captured a country house with long sloping lawns and trees to one side. In the foreground, taking up most of the shot, was the corner of a pool with lilies on its surface and reed beds along its banks. Three figures emerged as I studied it. On the lawn a woman ran towards the house, her head turned; the silhouette of a man filled one of the upper windows; and in the bottom right corner a fisherman cast into the pool from beside a boathouse. All of them looked out of the picture and into the room. I turned away and moved towards the window. The market was silent and the memory of the merry din I had just witnessed floated in my mind untethered.

I had an unnaturally early start in the morning. After washing, and smearing cream between my itching toes, I retrieved Dr Wistman's journal and climbed into bed with the generous balloon of brandy Elizabeth had poured. It was with distinct relief I neared the end of the journal. Hidden meanings were emerging. They were difficult to pin down and isolate. If I looked too closely, they collapsed into a blur, but they were there, fundamentally woven into the rhythm, structure, and tone of Alfred's text.

The physicists' first major achievement at Blackden Carr created much excitement for Alfred. In 1946 they constructed "the Speculum", the largest radio telescope in the world. Dr Wistman surrendered his Comb to their research, providing a perfect foundation and shape for their parabolic reflecting aerial. Following the line of Alfred's trenches, three miles of steel wire created a bowl 222 feet in diameter. Laid on its back, the bowl reflected radio waves up to a focal point suspended 159 feet above the ground by a hexagonal ring of scaffold poles.

Although it covered only a small strip of sky near its zenith, the Speculum provided readings from as far away as the Great Nebula in Andromeda, the first time a known extragalactic radio source had been detected. Alfred was mesmerised by this alchemy, the transformation of radiation into sound. For three years he listened with wonder to the music of the spheres – solar radio emissions, meteor trails and luminescent auroral clouds. Then, in 1950, the opportunity he had waited for finally presented itself. Wistman's excitement was physically rendered, his pen strokes bitten into the page.

"I could scarcely conceal my elation sitting at the back of the Park Royal Hut and listening to the discussion of their plans. Though unaware and unable to comprehend my studies, these astral engineers are connecting the strands of my Great Work. They are to search for an echo of that catalyst in Dee's understanding of the cosmos, the remnants of Tycho's Supernova. The date they have chosen could not be more significant - 21st December, the winter solstice, a night when the edges of things are their least rigid.

Dee could not have known what he was looking at when a new celestial body as bright as Jupiter appeared in the sky. We know now. A supernova is the death of a star, a massive explosion sending debris millions of miles through space. This is the Prima Materia; this oxygen, magnesium, silicon, calcium, and iron becomes new worlds, new plants, new animals. The matter that makes my body has changed and rearranged over billions of years and will continue to do so long after I am gone. Stars create life. When that life finishes, fungi transform it into something else. Is this not true alchemy?"

Wistman's words crept off the page, hyphal threads tangling themselves into my own story. I did not share his enthusiasm for the supernova making its way inevitably towards me. How he intended to harness the telescope's search for it was not clear from his journal. Alfred remained convinced that John Dee's *Mercurius Coelestis* contained the forgotten knowledge he needed to complete his work. Still unable to track it down, Alfred requested something else from the British Museum's archives, Dee's scrying glass, the black obsidian mirror through which he had glimpsed into other worlds.

"I underestimated the impact the arrival of this artefact would have on me. With an almost reverential awe I unpacked a small red crate marked with the Museum's stamp. I dug my hands into the sawdust and carefully removed a parcel bound with stiff brown paper, its wrapping held together by string. I placed it on the table and untied the bow. The paper opened like a flower. And there it was. I could only stare at it, unmoving. Dee saw on its surface things passed and things yet to happen. He used it to break down the barriers we have built around us, to converse with angels, to summon demons.

At last I lift it from the paper. The mirror is impossibly dark, as black as the ink on this page, and seems to vibrate in my hands, as if charged with a tiny electrical force. Roughly circular in shape, it is carved from volcanic rock, polished to reflect Dee's view of the world. The black mirror is older still, stolen from the Aztecs whose Priests used it to consult with their own Lord of Divination, Tezcatlipoca — 'the Smoking Mirror'.

Gazing upon that mirrored stone returns a silhouette sharp and clear but smooth and featureless, like an unfinished carving. It transforms my face, capturing my essence, my potential, rather than my physical form. As I try in vain to focus and refocus on the contours of my skull, I begin to slide into that black water, seeing through the mirror and beyond. I can be anyone now. Any thing. No longer must I wait for a miracle. I am the destroying angel. And perhaps I shall see her again."

There are no further entries, just blank pages and pressed flowers. What Alfred did with Dee's scrying glass in that dark Cheshire field is not clear. Who he had been before the war, before he scratched out his name and his history, remains a secret. I placed the journal and the empty brandy glass on the floor and switched off the bedside lamp. Lying there in the darkness at the edge of sleep, I had a curious notion. Reading Dr Wistman's journal was no longer a process of learning. It was one of remembering.

PART FOUR
THE STONES

"Altar, ingress, library. The circle has no end."
The Northern Antiquarian, Dr Merlyn Cullis, Village Archaeology
Press

Addersmeat

Three stand around the well, hands joined. A triangle and a circle. They begin to turn, against the sun. Round and round. Faster and faster. Stone tips on its axis, back and forth, back and forth, striking the hexagon's edge. This ringing grows louder and louder, faster and faster. Three become a blur, like wind, and rise from the ground. Triangle, circle, hexagon. Stone glows, brighter and brighter. The needle twitches and in brilliant light a figure calls to me.

"I'm here."

I reach out but he is too faint.

"It's time."

I open my eyes, sat up, arms outstretched. I am crying. I do not know where I am, or why I am here.

"Be downstairs in fifteen minutes. I'll not be dallying."

There had been no time for breakfast. There had barely been time to dress and gather my things. The suspension on the Land Rover was shot, the seats hard. I bounced up and down as the landlord sped along black narrow lanes, the bruise on my knee throbbing like a beacon.

"Could we slow down a little?"

My words faded into the roar of the engine. We lurched around a blind corner, tyres locking on ice. The Land Rover's bare metal door struck my hip with a crack. I winced in pain and held on to darkness as we rushed down the tunnel of the truck's headlamps. Eventually the lane climbed steeply between tall wintry hedges, and we began to slow.

"I'll thank you not to discuss my personal circumstances with your staff."

"I don't follow."

"I think you do."

The landlord took his eyes from the road and looked at me blankly.

"My father."

"I don't know your father."

"His passing."

"I'm sorry to hear that. You have my sympathies."

He turned away and pulled something from his jacket.

"Where did you get that?

"The lip of the well."

I snatched Dad's compass from his hand and nodded grudgingly.

"Costermonger's been round. I've made you a docky."

The landlord flicked on an overhead light and pointed downwards. On the floor between us was a large wicker basket. I lifted a corner of the cloth cover and peered beneath. Inside I could see six hard boiled eggs, a large pie, two apples, and an enormous slab of fruit cake.

We pulled up at a pair of giant gates set back a little from the lane. The ironwork was expertly wrought into a woodland scene. Weaved into the intricate canopy was a parliament of metal rooks. The vertical bars were gnarled tree trunks with flowers and mushrooms decorating their base. Stone walls rose up on either side of the gates. They were tall, some seven or so feet in height. The headlamps picked out a large flat stone carved with the words "ROOKSNEST MANOR". Wind and rain had sunk and stretched the letters, merging the two O's into a single, larger hole. After unlocking a series of chains and sliding open a great bolt, the landlord forced the heavy iron doors open with the weight of his shoulder before climbing back into the truck.

Snowdrops

Fresh snowfall covered the grounds, and the tyres made a satisfying crunch as we made our way slowly up the drive. Rooksnest was sunk into a hollow at the foot of the moors; in the early morning gloom those dark ridges of wild land loomed over the house like black waves forever at the point of collapse. Brakes of rhododendron spilled onto the drive creating a series of narrow canyons, grasping at the sides of the truck. Dead blossom decorated the frozen branches, a pale blur of purples, whites, and yellows, glowing softly in the headlamps.

The landlord continued cautiously along the drive before turning the truck around where the bushes thinned out, twenty yards or so from the house. After switching off the ignition he sat motionless in his seat, staring silently through the headlamps. Several seconds passed and I looked down awkwardly at my watch. I had forgotten to set and wind it.

"Do you know what time it is?"

"We'll find out when we get inside."

"But you are wearing a watch?"

Without replying, the landlord pulled a torch out the glove box and handed it to me. After climbing down from the Land Rover, he faded into darkness. The boot opened and closed, and he reappeared at the window, tapping on the glass with the head of an axe, before vanishing again, up onto the roof. There was a brilliant flash, and I covered my eyes. When I opened them, the landlord had angled spotlights on top of the truck to illuminate the house. I jumped down with my bag and the basket and followed his shadow along a white corridor of light.

Despite being partially boarded, Rooksnest was a not unattractive Georgian manor house. It was modest and understated, as if awed by the dramatic moorland surrounding it. Planks sealed shut the front door. On either side two giant stone rooks stood guard, their heads turned to observe visitors. Lit by the truck's spotlights, the house had a two-dimensional quality, like it was a façade, or an illustration cut from a book. I dropped the bag and the basket on the frozen gravel and climbed three worn steps leading up to the door. The landlord stared at me before spitting on the ground.

"Stand back."

"Can I help?"

He looked me up and down.

"I'm not sure you're able to provide much of that."

I stepped to one side, quietly seething. The landlord raised the heavy axe over his head and brought it violently down on the planks nailed across the shallow porch. The dark silence of that place was at once shattered by the dreadful cracking and splintering of old wood. It was a terrible noise, strange and high-pitched like a scream. I instinctively raised my arms to my face and staggered backwards down the steps as wooden daggers tore through the air. A small shard caught me on the back of my left hand and buried itself in the flesh. I responded with a squeal of pain. The landlord stopped chopping and laid his axe on the ground. He walked down the steps and grabbed my left wrist.

"You don't want to be going in there with that wound."

"Don't be silly, it's nothing."

"Didn't sound like nothing."

"It took me by surprise that's all."

"I think we should leave."

"That's absurd. I've work to do."

He stared at me impassively, still holding my wrist. I knew I was not strong enough to break free of his grip and did not want the humiliation of failing to wriggle out.

"Do you mind?"

At last he let go, picked up the axe and completed his destruction of the planks. I hung back and gently worked the splinter from my hand as blood dripped a pattern of red dots into the snow.

Forget-me-not

"Are you coming in?"

The landlord answered by remaining at the bottom of the steps and staring up at a wilting holly wreath hanging limply from the door. I flicked on my torch and stepped into the dark hallway. You were greeted by an enormous portrait hanging from the wall. Its subject was handsome in that military way, with thick brilliantined hair, a spectacular Kitcheneresque moustache and an unflinching stare. At first glance he radiated an intimidating power and authority, but before long his expression betrayed something less certain. It was perhaps discomfort or frustration. No, not that. It was closer to pain. He looked trapped.

"Who's that?"

The landlord could not see the painting from where he stood and made no effort to bring it into his line of sight.

"No-one that should still be here."

I stepped back out of the hall and stood in the doorway.

"I was told you'd be able to provide me some local history, context for the collection as it were."

"Is that so?"

"It is yes. You are being employed by the library are you not?"

"That's Mr Woodlock, a millowner from Manchester. Used to own Rooksnest before. He's not remembered kindly."

"How so?"

"He was hunted. Saw his wife drown and couldn't escape. They reckon he killed his daughter after that. Threw her from the upstairs window."

"What became of him?"

"Went to the trenches, never came back."

"And what about a man by the name of Wistman?"

The landlord did not answer.

"Was he from round here too? …Well?"

"He sometimes has a stall on the market."

"Really? And his father ran the stall before him? And perhaps his father's father before that?"

"No fathers, no. Wistman's always been here."

"When is he around?"

"Not seen him for a long while. He's an eelworm that one."

"What do you mean?"

"He keeps what he catches."

"I don't understand."

"No, you don't. I'll be back at two to collect."

"What's that? Two o'clock? That's a little early. I understand there's a significant amount of work to be done."

"Work?"

"Yes, work. Cataloguing and such like."

"It'll be two or no time at all. Come out through the gate and wait on the lane. I might not find you again if I have to come back in."

"What is this? I was led to believe the library were paying you for the entire day."

"Seems you've been led to believe a number of things."

"Can I ring you at lunch time, let you know how I'm getting on?"

"There's no telephoning here. It's a dead zone."

"Well I'll be damned! You are being particularly unhelpful."

"Can't help with no dead zone."

"You know what, forget it. I'll stay the night. But believe me, I'll be reporting this to the library and making sure it's taken from your wages."

"I wouldn't do that if I were you."

His face was without expression. It was blank not from ignorance as I had conceitedly presumed. It was blank like a rock.

"Are you threatening me?"

"Wouldn't stay here."

"Nonsense! Scared of the dark are you?"

"It won't be dark tonight."

With that he turned away and I watched from the steps as he set off around the house. He stopped suddenly in his tracks, a black silhouette against the Land Rover's white spotlight, and looked upwards to the second-floor windows.

"I'll get the generator running and then I'm away. When it comes, don't let it in."

"When what comes?"

"It won't be what you hope."

"What are you talking about?"

"It's up to you how you play your role."

"Why do you people speak in riddles?"

"If you find your senses, I'll be outside the gate at two. I'll not be dallying."

The landlord shouted over the crack of splintering wood, like a tree losing its branch to a storm. He ignored it and disappeared into the darkness.

The carousel

My instructions from William described Rooksnest as a Georgian manor house later converted into a medical institute. The dark hallway greeting me showed no sign of the house having been anything other than a family home, suddenly vacated many years ago. Beneath a skin of dust, the walls were decked with sagging, faded ribbons, and withered mistletoe. I tentatively reached out and touched one of those ghost berries and it burst in a tiny cloud of white smoke. Shining the torch downwards revealed an army of wooden Nutcrackers, marching along each side of the hall towards the foot of a great sweeping staircase. I followed them hesitantly to their destination. It reared up from the ground to the ceiling of the floor above, the terrible skeleton of a giant spruce, decorated with rotting wooden toys, broken glass baubles, and chains of tarnished golden bells flickering sadly in the pale beam. At the foot of the tree was a pile of unopened presents, covered in a blanket of yellow pine needles. The smell of dust and stagnant air was overwhelming. Beneath that decay was something else.

William's notes suggested I would find the books stored in plastic crates in a common room at the back of the house. I knew before I opened the door that no such room existed. In its place was a large old-fashioned library. Deep red mahogany shelves ran from floor to ceiling and covered most of the walls. The middle of the room contained further stacks arranged in diagonal lines to match the tessellation in the parquet floor. Every shelf, wherever you looked, was tightly packed with books. There was no chance my work could be completed in three days. I was going to be here forever.

The landlord had apparently got the generator going, though the lamps in the library provided little radiance. I walked up and down the length of the shelves; it was difficult to know where to start. Books did not appear to be in any particular order. If they were, they were organised into a system beyond my comprehension. I selected the desk by the windows overlooking the lawn. There was a curious black scorch mark in the wood, recalling William's account of the desk at Chetham's. After rifling through my bag, I arranged its contents neatly before me – a blank logbook, Dr Wistman's journal, my father's compass, and the torch the landlord had given me. I pulled down on the string of a green glass lamp sat on the desk and scanned the list of titles William had instructed me to look for. One entry was underlined and punctuated by two question marks, "*Mercurius Coelestis*, John Dee, 1597". I felt a jolt of excitement. Whether it was my own, or William's, or Alfred's, I cannot say.

It was cold in the library, and my lungs protested with faint silver clouds. I kept on my coat and fished the gloves out the pockets. Until the room warmed up, I would have to keep active, so I began to empty the shelves and pile the books in stacks on the desk.

There was no catalogue for the collection. The books were wild, feral things. I captured every title in the blank logbook William had provided, before returning them to the shelves, which I labelled with stickers and carefully mapped. For some while I worked in a slightly hazy murk. The only sign of dawn on this shortest day had been a soft red glow behind the moorland towering over the house. As soon as the sun climbed over the crest of the hills, light poured down the valley and funnelled into a beam that burst through the glass doors and into the library, illuminating something placed on an old tea wagon parked against the far wall.

The sun was most peculiarly channelled, as if the landlord's truck were shining its spotlight into the room. I closed the book I was studying and followed the white shaft across the parquet floor. Its focus was covered by a shawl, hiding what appeared to be a bird cage. I lifted the covering carefully to find a large, ornate carousel with a bright red hexagonal canopy. Beneath it was a woodland scene, with six stags frozen in mid-flight. Upon the back of each stag sat a small girl, their frightened porcelain faces rendered with an unnerving accuracy, magnified by the sun's brilliance. I gazed at the detail of their features for some time before jumping backwards with a start. The carousel had exploded into life. The stags galloped violently through the trees in pursuit of a fleeing boar. A familiar melody drifted between the branches, beautiful but persistent, driving the herd on its charge. I don't know how long I gazed at it, but it stopped as suddenly as it began, and the rays of light that had brought it to life burst apart, flooding the room with morning.

Congelation

I re-covered the carousel with the shawl and moved back to the windows overlooking the garden. I opened the glass doors and stepped out onto a white blanket of frozen snow. A pool of mist heaved and sighed gently over this blank page, a haze-fire glimmering softly in the dawn light. Every surface was sealed in a brilliant skin of ice. Here and there it melted upwards in twisting columns, as the sun's fingers tightened their grip.

The lawn swept downwards into a patch of heavier mist, marshland perhaps. Behind this, woodland stretched up the moors beyond. Rooksnest was at the crossroads of several steep valleys and the hills climbed overhead in every direction. The ice covering them sparkled in the sunshine like glass, as if the estate were housed in its own display case.

One side of the garden was edged by a spinney of five giant ash trees. They shifted and squirmed with the scores of rooks hopping between their naked branches, blackening as snow slipped off in silent cascades. On the opposite edge stood the probable cause of the sun's strange channelling into the library, a magnificent four-stone dolmen, surrounded by frozen heather.

Fresh snowfall and swirling mist cloaked the gardens with ambiguity, according them an ill-defined quality, like a distant memory, or a paling dream. Only the stones existed with any certainty. The three uprights and their capstone sparkled like stars beneath the sea. With each soft muffled step across the lawn, the dolmen grew more beautiful. The frost on the stone shimmered, and the stone beneath the frost shimmered, and the stone beneath the stone shimmered. Gneiss is an ancient rock subjected to unimaginable heat and pressure that has left it banded and rich in quartz. This quartz caught the early morning sun and splintered it into hundreds of tiny flashes of light, amplified along the feathery crystals of hoar frost exploding from the stone.

Sudden movement at the end of the garden interrupted my thoughts. I watched as a figure emerged from the trees beyond the marsh. He was carrying fishing tackle and making his way carefully to what looked like an old boathouse enmired in the mud. Stopping suddenly in his tracks he turned to face me, his form quivering in the shifting mist. Neither of us moved. After several moments with our gazes locked, I slowly raised my hand to wave. He lowered his head and his eyes flashed silver before I saw the rods he held in the air were antlers, tangled with leaves and grasses. The stag sniffed something on the breeze before turning his giant head and fading slowly back into the woods. Somewhere in the distance a cuckoo called. It was too late in the year. Perhaps I was mistaken.

Cibation

Daunting though it was, cataloguing the collection filled me with an enormous sense of calm and wellbeing. I glided along the shelves in a dream-like trance, stripping out books and piling them on the desk. Titles stored higher up could be reached via a set of wheeled wooden steps with its own handrail. I took great delight in utilising that tiny staircase whenever necessary, and indeed unnecessary. Existence had been reduced to this one room. My work was bringing order and meaning, linking those disparate ideas and memories into a coherent whole. Through the pleasure of repetition and detail I could feel myself slipping from the real world. I was happy.

Beyond the library time passed. Without a working watch, my only measure was the journey of the low sun across the December sky. That and my belly. I had made a promise with myself to ignore hunger until I discovered a title from William's list. Before I lifted the picnic basket onto the desk, I had removed and catalogued five books of significant rarity and value, early editions of works and illustrations by Albrecht Durer, Michael Scot, Robert Fludd and Roger Bacon. The final book was a first edition of a WB Yeats collection, its pages unfortunately stained by some dark liquid.

The lunch prepared by the landlord was excellent. As well as two boiled eggs and a slice of fruit cake, I managed a quarter of the pie, possibly the best I have tasted. Pork, venison, and oyster mushrooms filled the thick golden pastry, a perfect balance of flavours and texture. I washed it down with a flask of white beer. The beer was weak, but wonderfully sweet and refreshing.

At the bottom of the basket, I found something else, a rod of some description, bound in white cloth. I placed it on the desk and unrolled the thin linen covering to find a short wooden cane with a rowan shaft. The handle was bulb-shaped and made from solid, hallmarked silver. It was finely smithed into an oak tree, its intricate roots twisting delicately round and down the shaft. Narrowing to a point, the tip was iron, hard and heavy and black. It was a peculiar item, too short to be a walking stick for anyone other than a small child. It was more likely a truncheon, or an angler's priest. The age, craftsmanship and generous use of silver suggested the cane was of considerable value and I wondered how it had ended up with my lunch. I rolled it back into the linen and returned it to the picnic basket with the remains of my provisions.

Hide and seek

Disturbing the rhythm of cataloguing invited the world back into focus. Until then I had managed to put the house from my mind. Now that curiosity had woken up, the thought of all those unopened doors and the rooms behind them quickly grew into an unwelcome itch.

Ignoring downstairs, I climbed up the oak staircase that swept around the skeleton of the giant Christmas tree. At the top, attached to the panelled wall, were six infantry swords, arranged into two intersecting triangles, creating a star with a hexagonal centre. They were flanked by the mounted heads of a giant stag and a fearsome-looking boar.

...74...75...76...

I counted every step from the library in my head, unconsciously mapping the layout of the house. Opening out in both directions around the stairs, the upper landing had numerous doors coming off it, more doors it seemed than there was space for rooms. The first few I tried were locked.

…95…96…97…

I was about to abandon my exploration when at last one of the handles gave and the door began to creak open. Instead of marching straight in I paused. There was a noise coming from inside, like the thud of furniture on a wooden floor. It scraped and rattled and banged, but quietly, as if it were happening at the other end of an enormously long room. I opened the door another inch or so and the noise immediately stopped. This was worse. Whatever was creating that sound had become aware of my presence. And it was listening, just behind the door.

…98…99…100. I'm coming, ready or not.

I took a deep breath and burst into the room.

It was empty in there, save for a small iron bed, an enamel sink and a cracked mirror resting against the wall. Other than a trace of dry rot in the beams and a noticeable drop in temperature, it was all perfectly unremarkable. There was no evidence there had been anything in there making that strange noise and I happily assumed it was rats in the walls, or birds in the roof space, more acceptable propositions than the images that had flashed briefly across my mind.

I approached the window and looked out over the lawns sparkling with frozen snow. With the mist lifted I could see over to the paddock beyond the ash trees. I watched through the frosted glass as six stags stood up at once and crossed the white field in a line. They reached a grid of red walls in the centre and began to circle it, round and round, against the sun. As the carousel turned, I could hear that music again, drifting slowly up through the house. I gazed transfixed at this strange coil of antler and fur until a car engine from the other side of the house diverted my attention.

I left the room and headed along the landing to a tall window on the opposite side of the staircase. A veil of mist hung heavily over the front of the house. Everything beyond the gate was blanked out. I looked down and watched the landlord stroll into view in front of his Land Rover. It surely wasn't two o'clock already. The landlord stopped suddenly in his tracks and turned his head, staring up at me. I waved, somewhat sheepishly. He did not wave back. He appeared to be talking to someone unseen, though I could not make out what they were saying. I tried to slide open the sash window, but it was stuck fast in its frame. After a short while I gave up and pressed my ear against the thin glass. *I'll not be dallying,* was all I caught from the landlord, before he strode off round the house and out of sight.

Satisfied I would be spending the night at Rooksnest, it would have been churlish not to inform the landlord I wasn't looking for a ride back into town. By the time I got down the staircase and out onto the drive however, neither he nor his truck were anywhere to be seen. The landlord does like to advertise he's not one for dallying. I guess he is a man of his word.

Hexenring

Instead of returning to cataloguing, I wandered round to the back of the house. The dolmen's quartz shimmered in the sun like frozen points of light. I stepped across the lawn and pushed my way through the tangle of heather. Between the pink flowers and the rocks was a ring of thawed earth, blackened by fire. The three standing stones were unusually tall, and I could stand up straight beneath the giant capstone. I tilted my head upwards and gazed at the rock hovering above my face. It was ellipse in shape, a great eye looking up at the stars. Its surface was carved with cups and rings and painted with a kaleidoscope of different lichens, Gold Dust, Moonglow and Sunburst. One carving stood out from the rest, a pattern of circles, a star within a flower. I could have lost myself there, but the stones reminded me of Dad, and I slipped into a familiar melancholy.

This hard blank silence grew and twisted until it became something else, a faint but excited shrieking. I turned around and looked out across the lawn. Before the paddock at the edge of the garden was a log store and a number of felled trunks. In front of them a cloak of rooks swarmed over something piled up in the snow. There was a hypnotic fluidity to it, like watching a thing burn with cold black flames. The scores of birds obscured their prey, and I assumed it was a large animal carcass. Sudden horror unfolded a lifeless arm and dropped it heavily onto the white lawn. In a frenzy now, the rooks were a dark fire of wing and beak and claw. I was mesmerised, unable to look away. All at once the rooks fell still and turned towards me. They stared at my motionless figure for several moments before a merlin dropped on them like a rock into floodwater. The rooks took off at once, flickering away over the marsh. They left in their place a small heap of bodies and the stink of rotting flesh. My hand throbbed. With the spell broken I realised I had been picking at the splinter wound and blood was trickling down my wrist. I gathered my thoughts and stepped out from beneath the capstone. The memory of a rabbit crisscrossed the lawn, scores of tiny faces screaming into the snow. These distinctive tracks carved the frozen garden into geometric shapes. Intrigue fought with fear as I followed a line to the log store.

Relief escaped as a misty cloud in the cold air. I had not heard my own laughter for a long time, and it choked off as quickly as it begun. The corpses I had watched the rooks tear apart were three scarecrows, dumped in a tangle of limbs. There was no blood, or bones, or strips of flesh, only straw and sticks and shredded cloth. It seemed they had fallen victims of folklore, compelled to dance until they collapsed with exhaustion. They lay in a faerie ring, a red circle of geometrically latticed mushrooms pushing their way up through the snow. This explained the smell. Red cage is as malodorous as it is beautiful. In England, it is more commonly known as the basket stinkhorn, though I prefer the sinister poetry of its French name, Coeur de Sorcière - "the witch's heart". It was unusual to see them so late in the year.

This damp edge of the lawn was rich with fungi. Clumps of sticky, shiny mushrooms grew at the base of the logs where they were protected from the snow. Rhizomorphs coiled around the felled trunks, a complex network of black tendrils reaching out in every direction. It looked like honey fungus, and I almost willed the night to come. The fruiting body can display bioluminescence, responding to the stars with an aquamarine glow. It is known as foxfire, a phenomenon I had read about with fascination but never witnessed.

One of the trunks in the log pile was recently felled. It was bound in metal chains and mottled with some dark liquid. I looked towards the copse of ash further down the lawn. Adjacent trees had braided together, their cambia grafting into single limbs until the end of one ash and the beginning of another was unclear. It created a perfect wooden arch in the centre of the spinney. At the near edge a jagged stump yawned from the earth. I had enjoyed last night's unusual celebrations, but seeing that great ash torn apart from its family nudged my imagination somewhere else. I looked away with a vague sadness and into the paddock beyond. In the centre of the field was the sandstone pinfold I had observed from the upstairs window. Small black hills made a ring around this enclosure, the earth turned upside down. Those blind tunnellers had not dared stray beneath the lawn, cautiously heeding the warning spelled out on the metal fence. A dozen moles were strung up, twisted into new shapes by fungi and bacteria. They were arranged at different heights along the rails, musical notes scoring their own death. I shivered and returned at once to the house.

PART FIVE
THE HUNT

"It cannot be that a thing happens and then happens no more. Once it happens, it happens forever, and so it has always happened."

Mercurius Coelestis, John Dee (translated by H. Grimsditch)

Sublimation

For the remainder of the afternoon, I faded into the shelves as the watery sun slipped quietly towards the horizon. I forgot why I was supposed to be there and lost myself in reading. You could argue that over the course of my relatively short life I have done little and read a lot. Some might look down on this imbalance, but my imagination doesn't distinguish between the two inputs. Experience is experience, it cares not whether this is mine or someone else's.

The library's collection was fascinating, a treasury of outdated theories, biographies of old orders, religious texts, studies of demonology and witchcraft, alchemical recipes, folklore, superstition, and grimoires. Dad would have loved it. Overtaken by a compulsion to learn things, I selected books from the shelves at random and pored over them. The library was a memory of shifting beliefs, and I was reminded of Wistman's assertion that magic never went away.

It was a whiff of cigarette smoke that eventually broke the spell.

"Hello?"

I closed the book I was reading and placed it gently down on the desk.

"Is anyone there?"

My words came out dry and a little cracked, as if reluctant to reveal themselves. I held my breath and strained my ears, listening for a sound. It was low and muffled, but I would swear I heard footsteps making their way up the staircase. There was no reason I should be alone in the house – maybe it was a groundsman, the landlord, or even the Head Librarian late for our appointment – and yet the idea of meeting someone else made me uncomfortable. Without thinking, I rifled through the picnic basket and pulled out the rowan cane. As I unwound its linen wrap, I could hear a faint irregular ticking. I looked down at the desk. The needle of Dad's compass twitched erratically. Grasping tightly onto the tip of the cane, I struck the silver handle against my other hand, drawing strength from the cold iron against my skin.

I left the library and made my way between the army of Nutcrackers in the hallway. At the foot of the staircase, I froze. There was a girl at the top pointing down at me. She opened her mouth as if to scream. I backed away and she collapsed into a dark puddle. This shadow stretched up to the head of the stag attached to the wall on the landing above. I laughed unconvincingly and climbed the steps towards it.

Starting at the small open bedroom, I moved along the landing. There were eight other doors, all of them locked. I pressed my ear against their dark wood panels. There was no sign anyone was behind them. Having completed a full circuit, I found myself back at the open bedroom. I pushed the door gently with the cane and stepped inside. Save for the bed, the sink, and the mirror leaning against the wall, the room was still empty. I followed a series of large, muddy boot prints around the bed and up to the window. Carved into the sill was the same pattern I had seen on the capstone of the dolmen, a series of interlocking circles making a star within a flower. I peered through the dim glass to the marsh at the end of the lawn. Beyond that, trees pushed out in every direction and crept up the moors. A thin smoke column twisted through that canopy of frosted green and collapsed into the grey sky.

Turning away from the window, I caught a glimpse of myself in the mirror resting against the wall. The glass was cracked along the bottom, revealing the underside of the bed. A pair of eyes watched me from the shadows. It was difficult to see from that angle, but there was the outline of a shape hiding there, whimpering softly. Instead of eliciting sympathy from me, I was suddenly overtaken by anger and strode across the room towards it. The crying grew louder, and my rage intensified. I thrust my hand down into the darkness and quickly yanked it out again, roaring with pain and fury. Sunk into the skin was a deep bite mark. It had reopened the splinter wound, stretching it out into a ragged, bloody circle. Overwhelmed by violence, I swung the cane wildly beneath the bed, clattering it furiously against the frame and the floorboards. Eventually I stopped, exhausted, and slowly lowered my head to look. There was nothing there beside the charred remains of a small log.

Hatred quickly drained away, but my body shook vigorously, and my breathing was quick and short. The back of my hand was bleeding heavily so I made my way downstairs to the library and grabbed the cane's linen wrap. I bound it carefully around the wound and watched as blood pooled in that curious burn mark on the desk.

Eating the dead

The sky leadened over the gardens outside and I continued to pull books off the shelves. I flicked absently through their contents and entered them into the catalogue, but it no longer afforded me the same joy. It was automatic now and I had to remind myself why I was there and what I was doing.

I would have ignored what happened upstairs, but for the throbbing pain in the back of my hand. It must have been an animal of some kind. The bite radius was too big for a rat. It must have been a fox. That was it, a fox. Dad once told me the vixen call is often mistaken for the cries of a small child. If I kept the bandage tightly wrapped, I could overlook the distinctly human teeth marks sunk into my skin.

Eventually I got up from the desk and wandered between the stacks without purpose. There was a tension in the room making me claustrophobic. It was as if the library had grown smaller, no longer able to accommodate its own contents. This impossible hypothesis was confirmed by a row of books out of sorts with those around them. Carefully I removed six volumes of an encyclopaedia pushing their way over the edge of the shelf. Concealed behind them I found a cork-stoppered bottle filled with brown translucent liquid. As my fingers closed around it, a toenail tangled in hair nudged gently against the inside of the glass. I snatched my hand away and jammed the books back in place. I was beginning to regret my decision to stay the night at Rooksnest and considered the cosy lounge of the Drab Tooth with something like nostalgia.

I returned to the desk and fiddled absently with the bandage around my hand. The wound beneath it continued to throb. It was so quiet in the library I could almost hear it, see it even, transmitting signals out into the world. I was reminded of Dad's work at Fylingdales, and the messages intercepted by those giant spheres squatting on the moors. What if something were listening to the echoes of my pain?

I tried to return to cataloguing. It will sound childish when you read this back, but I felt the books were conspiring against me. They had been startled at first and allowed themselves to be controlled. As they got the measure of me, they grew more stubborn. Titles blurred and spines crumbled at the lightest touch. Other books were packed so tightly they refused to yield from the shelf. Even the shelves resisted, shedding the labels I had assigned them and leaving curled stickers scattered across the parquet floor like leaves.

And there was something else. I got up from the desk and poked around once more. Although I had previously overlooked the fresh pile of logs in the fireplace, the library was as close to normal as it could be. I was about to dismiss this intangible apprehension as fatigue when I looked out into the garden. Ropes were attached to three of the ash trees. At the bottom of each swung a scarecrow, hanged by its neck. Their rhythmic swaying in the gentle breeze triggered an instinctive sense of dread and I stared at those straw corpses unthinking, hollowed out by a cold fear. When that empty space became filled, I found myself overwhelmed with anger. This is why the landlord had returned, not to bring me back into town, but to punish me, in retribution for my threat to have his wages docked. I grabbed the torch from the desk and burst out through the glass doors onto the lawn.

"Show yourself. I know you're there."

The garden was silent and still, as if the outside were not expecting me. I strode out across the white lawn towards the ash trees, the frozen grass twinkling in the owl light.

"Have you nothing better to do with your time? It's pathetic."

Though the pallid sun still bled over the moors, the canopy of trees was black like midnight. This concentrated darkness twisted and flickered as the rooks hopped from branch to branch. I clicked on the torch and waved it across the figures strung from the gloom. They were all women, and of different age. Stitched onto cloth sack faces, their expressions portrayed an unsettling mix of terror, pain, and anger, and possessed a detail that seemed disproportionate to their function. A callow fear made me look down at my feet. They had left an impression in the snow, long strides out from the library doors. Other than the prickings of rabbits and hares, there was no evidence anyone else had been here.

Casting the torch across the ash trees revealed something else, lesions, dark and diamond-shaped, scarring the trunks where they forked. The trees' crowns were stripped, and recent growth restricted to the lower branches. Any leaves clinging stubbornly on into winter were as black as pitch. Witch's brooms erupted from the canopy; dense shoot tangles crafted by the rooks into nests. The trees were suffering from dieback. Leaf litter caught in the roots obscured the trees' killer, a fungus quietly releasing its spores. This slow corruption is creeping through the branches, choking the flow of water until the trees die of thirst, their ancient strength tricked into the darkness.

Sudden movement from the paddock catches me off guard. A dark shape shifts between the pinfold walls. Though difficult to make out in the half-light of dusk, it looks like a large pig. I shine the torch towards it but its soft beam refuses to cross the field. Low snorts and heavy breathing suggest the creature is wounded. I shiver. It has grown cold. Deep within the woods the wind roars. I glance behind me as I hurry back inside. The honey fungus is beginning to glow.

Jacob's Ladder

There was no dramatic flare of doomfire. The sun retreated without protest, eager to escape this longest night. Darkness was sealing shut the library; the only illumination came from the desk lamp and the dim lights attached to the walls. It was even blacker outside. When I stood before the glass doors and looked out onto the garden, there was no answer, just my muted face staring back at me, sockets black. That someone could be watching, hidden behind my own reflection, filled me with unease.

I moved away from the windows and made myself more comfortable in the wing-backed armchair beside the fireplace. The logs in the hearth required some effort to get going. When at last they caught, the flames danced and crackled pleasingly.

Sipping from a flask of beer, I sank slowly into the leather chair and thumbed absently through a stack of books placed on the small table beside me. The warmth of the fire and the flickering words hung heavy on my tired eyes, which crossed and closed as I made my way through the pile. The book at the bottom was old. It was limply bound, a single piece of plain vellum with Yapp edges, wrapped around and sealed shut with tarnished metal clasps. Its simplicity marked it out from the lavish gold tooling and gilt lettering that adorned many of the other books in the library. Carefully I slid open the two copper hooks.

Immediately my breathing quickened, and my hands began to tremble. At first glance I was not prepared to accept what I was holding. I read the title over and over. Wistman had searched for it endlessly and failed. William doubted that it even existed. But I had found it.

Mercurius Coelestis is a dizzying collection of alchemical diagrams, rituals, rites and summonings. The heavens are beautifully rendered amongst comets and stars, the earth decorated with stags and boars and flowers. Its goatskin pages are separate leaves of varying size, stitched together and removable from the cover. Written in Latin and Coptic, Dee's text was incomprehensible to me. Foolscap inserts tell the story, handwritten translations signed at the bottom – *Ms. H. Grimsditch*.

I lost track of time studying Dee's practices. There was little in his process I could consciously understand, but at the very edge of my comprehension something was starting to flicker. When I reached the last page, the room slipped away. Ms. Grimsditch's notes translated Dee's infamous experiment from his quarters at Manchester's cathedral college. They described how he summoned a demon on the table of the Audit room, how it scorched a mark in the oak desk, and how in mortal fear Dee sent it screaming back to hell. On the final page is Dee's rendering of the ritual and I stared at it in disbelief, my mind beginning to yaw and pitch. Dee sits at a desk, in a room surrounded by books. On the desk he has arranged a large hexagon of flower petals. Dee leans back in his chair, clutching his scrying glass, his face etched with fear. In the centre of the petals stands a demon. It does not share the traditionally grotesque characteristics of a medieval devil. This demon is of human form and curiously modern-looking. He cuts a rather awkward, stooped figure, as if uncomfortable in his body. His grey hair is straight and long and partly covers his eyes, which are sunk into a thin skeletal face. The skin is pale, particularly above his mouth, and he wears a long khaki trench coat, lined with a hexagonal print. Pinned to his chest is a large golden bee.

Wilde Jagd

Fear takes my hand and drags me out the chair. I stagger over to the glass doors. My reflection shines, three emeralds illuminating the sky. It is the glow of fungus surely, a magnificent foxfire, more brilliant than I could have imagined. There is something else though. Within the centre of each light burns a shadow, a human shadow. And they are moving.

Three women replace the scarecrows. They are hanged by their necks and engulfed by green flames. Their bodies twist and writhe in silent agony. I think perhaps they have always been here. I shut my eyes. Maybe the vision will fade. Their screams begin the moment they're gone, sound itself torn apart. I open my eyes and it stops. I turn away. The stench of rotting flesh makes my stomach turn.

I swallow down rising panic. I must be firm. I grab Dr Wistman's journal from the desk and march over to the hearth. With sudden violence I tear the pages out one by one and cast them into the fire. I feel no shame for destroying the only record of Alfred's work at Blackden Carr. Pages burn quickly with a curious grey flame and the faint hint of sulphur. White smoke creeps up and out into the room like a fret. It is strangely translucent, and granular, more like a cloud of tiny spores. The mist begins to glow. Within this pale light is the outline of a figure. My heart makes a sudden joyful lurch.

Nearing the end of the journal I stop tearing and carry the book over to the desk. Carefully I remove the pages pressed with a flower, discarding the waxen leaves that protect them. Finishing with the yarrow, I arrange the thirteen pages in a neat pile on the desk. I unwrap the linen cloth binding my hand. The bite mark is raw and circular, with black tendrils reaching out to my fingers and wrist. I plunge my right thumb into the hole and twist. I let out a gasp as blood pours out, boring a red hole through the flowers. The corners of the library begin to flatten until there is no space between the shelves and I am outside.

Pale mist follows me across the frozen lawn and unfurls into the night air, drawing in the snow. Beyond it the stars and the black winter sky flee rapidly towards the horizon. The pursuing mist grows at an impossible rate, until the sky and the earth become the same. It boils and thickens into heavy clouds that flash and strobe with sharp white sparks. I can taste the lightning on my tongue.

Thunder grows, louder and louder. It shifts from an amorphous low rumble into a distinct sequence of sounds. Giant stags and monstrous hounds charge through galloping wind, churning the belly of the clouds with their pounding feet. It echoes against the moors and rushes back along the valley in a wave of dark noise, knocking the breath from my lungs. The crash of hooves comes faster and harder, and the gabble is a ferocious roar. They close in, the scent of the kill driving them into a frenzy.

Multiplication

It is no longer dark. Not clear, like daylight. But nor is it night. The marsh at the boundary of the gardens is gone. A millpond again, it is black water and lilies. I cross the lawn to the dolmen. I look at the stones for the first time, fossilised shadows of things we have forgotten how to see. They sing to me, a song without words. The pale mist covers me in a fine grey powder that leaves an electrical charge on my skin. There is a pressure in my ears. From beneath my tongue saliva is sucked to the roof of my mouth and the liquid in my eyes bleeds out at the corners.

I circle the stones six times, against the sun, tangling them in a hexagon of pressed flowers. Still holding the yarrow, I step into the dolmen and sit cross-legged on the floor beneath the capstone. I pull Dad's compass from my trouser pocket. Using the thin tapered edge, I scratch the dried petals from the page. The flower lifts itself from the paper as a cloud of dust. Not dust. Finer than that. It is light. Brilliant light. Bound with blood. Hanging beneath the capstone, it pulses and coruscates. It grows, painting the space between the stones. It is beyond the stones now. One by one it collects the hexagon of pressed flowers planted in the charred earth around me. They peel from their pages and burst in shimmering iridescent clouds. I am in the centre of the light as it spreads. The centre is everywhere. Within it grows the figure's outline, clearer and clearer. The coin strikes the water at the bottom of the rising well, and at last I make my wish.

Light gathers and narrows, burning brighter. It circles the stones, faster and faster. This dazzling whirlwind lifts me from the ground, drawing in, drawing out, particles and waves. I look down at my body. There is only light. My eyes are ablaze, but I feel nothing, hear nothing, see nothing. Nothing but light. The stones are not around me and above me, they are inside me, and I inside them. And the roots. And the stars. The cold mirror of my brain is seared away. Everything passes through. Moments gone, moments still to come. I can see it all, in the spaces between my bones. I am overwhelmed by the infinite beauty of everything, all at once. Until I see only horror.

Bursting into the sky the light releases me. It streaks across the heavens a comet, a prismatic, incandescent blaze of fire, burning away the pale mist. The air collapses into a million spores, filling the night with stars. Patterns on the stone are in the sky and patterns in the sky are on the stone, points of energy growing and contracting with my breath. The comet circles the dolmen in narrower and narrower gyres. Stars wheel around us, and all the sky turns. The air is riven with a terrible crack, knocking me onto the cold earth. The comet strikes the ground at the millpond's edge. Black water burns and becomes the night.

I lie, curled on the frozen grass, and watch through the rock. Light splinters cover the white lawn like broken glass. The ice in the trees is ringing, an echo of the market bells. No longer aflame the comet is a giant boar, caught and mortally wounded by the Hunt. A dagger pushes into its rib cage. Its snout is tied, its legs tangled in red. The carcass begins to twitch and squirm. These movements grow increasingly violent as the dead animal struggles back onto its feet. There is a guttural roar and the terrible sound of tearing skin. The belly of the pig opens like a pink flower and a figure claws its way out onto the lawn, grey and naked.

It is not him.

I have been tricked.

Projection

The capstone begins to sink. It is slow, almost imperceptible. Time pours out of me as it falls. Now I am a boy. I watch my self slip away, happy to become light. Stone and stars are inches above my face. I raise my hand and place it against a patch of pale lichen. It separates around my fingers and palm in tiny bright hexagons that draw me softly into the quartz. I wiggle my fingers and rock moves around them. I am absorbed, deeper and deeper into stone. Colder and darker, almost nothing. Stars. Hound. Tor. Coven. And then warmth. A large hand grips my wrist and drags me out onto the lawn.

I pull myself up from the ground a man again. His face is unformed, like outlines of my reflection in the scrying glass. But I know who it is. We hug and we weep and we laugh. And finally I let him go. I look down at my hands. I am holding the rowan cane.

The figure born from the boar's stomach drags itself towards the marsh. I follow, as yabbering rooks drop from the ash trees. They merge into one, a great black square that tries to swallow me. I swing the cane about my head. The dark mouth splinters again into birds. They continue to shriek and dive, and I tear at them with the rowan staff, its iron tip black lightning in the darkness. At last I reach the clawing figure. I slide my boot beneath his groin and roll him onto his back. His face is tightly skinned and pallid, especially above the mouth. A circular scar burns through his swollen belly. Empty sunken eyes stare up at me through strands of long grey hair. And the golden bee pinned into the bone of his chest shines brilliantly in the light of the burning sky.

I grip the cane tightly in both hands and hold it over him, knuckles paling. He smiles slowly and licks his grey upper lip. I raise the cane above my head and bring it down with all my might, thrusting the iron tip through his mouth. I feel the smash of his upper teeth, the piercing of the flesh at the back of his throat. The splintering of his skull. His head impaled on the white lawn.

His body rots at once, a bag of grey skin at my feet. I nudge it with my boot, and it bursts apart with a damp hiss. Nuts and berries and tiny shells spill out onto the ice. Clouds of petals float gently upwards into the midwinter sky. It leaves a paste on the frosted grass, soft and wet and clear. I watch as it tears and folds, stretching its way towards the millpond before sliding silently into that thick black water. It is dark as I pull the cane from the frozen earth. I turn around and go back to the library, back home.

Printed in Great Britain
by Amazon

37143329R10136